BOOKS BY IRENE BENNETT BROWN

Willow Whip

Morning Glory Afternoon

Before the Lark

BEFORE
THE
LARK

BEFORE
THE
LARK

840017

Irene Bennett Brown

ATHENEUM   1982   NEW YORK

LIBRARY OF CONGRESS CATALOGING IN PUBLICATION DATA

Brown, Irene Bennett.
Before the lark.

SUMMARY: In 1880's Missouri, hard-working twelve-year-old Jocey, tormented because of a disfiguring harelip, takes her ill grandmother to live on the farm her drifter father has abandoned.

[1. Farm life—Fiction.   2. Missouri—Fiction.
3. Harelip—Fiction.   4. Physically handicapped—Fiction]
I. Title.
PZ7.B81387Be   [Fic]   82-1729
ISBN 0-689-30920-1   AACR2

Published simultaneously in Canada by
McClelland & Stewart, Ltd.
Composition by American–Stratford Graphic Services, Inc.
Brattleboro, Vermont
Manufactured by Fairfield Graphics,
Fairfield, Pennsylvania
Designed by Felicia Bond
First Edition

 *to my beloved*

aquarian granddaughter,

Briana M

BEFORE
THE
LARK

CHAPTER 1

Like a tired beetle the two-wheeled laundry cart pulled by the bony horse crawled through the mud of the Kansas City, Missouri, street. On the cart's seat twelve-year-old Jocelyn Belle Royal shivered. "Thanks be," she said huskily to her horse, whose brown head came up and ears cocked back and forth. "No more laundry to deliver or pick up today, Nappy. It's suppertime. Let's go home to Gram."

Jocey added with affection, "You're a wise old friend, Napoleon. If I let you, you could take us home side streets and all, couldn't you? Without a word or a hand from me, and I could read my book." But for "The Chasers" she would try it. From long experience she knew that somewhere along the way they would appear and come after her.

Her hand shook as she snugged her ragged muffler closer about her dark head, making sure her mouth was covered. The Chasers, she thought with a sigh, made so much of her—flaw. Others did, too. Would anybody ever—sometime, somewhere—see past it to the real Jocey Royal?

Thinking about The Chasers had brought an icy knot to the pit of her stomach. Jocey took up her book and stroked the cover, in an attempt to ignore her fear. Here was the one way she could feel fine and good and lovely, losing herself in a romantic tale. This book was about a beautiful lady who lived in a mansion like those she delivered laundry to on Quality Hill. She liked to imagine though that it was not a book she was reading, but the life she was living. Snuggling her mind into that special life, Jocey began to read. After every few sentences, however, she lifted her head and she scanned her surroundings a second or two through worried, gray-violet eyes. So far, the enemy was nowhere to be seen.

Soon, the sharp March winds flipped the pages before she was ready to turn them. And the putrid smell of the stockyards to the west interfered with her concentration worse than a loud noise. Reluctantly, she allowed the wind to close her book. She could be beautiful, she could be the lady in the story, reading after supper tonight, maybe.

For now, she must put up with the real world: these Kaw River bottoms where she lived, and the close-by chokey stockyards and odorous rendering plants. No wonder Gram was sick. What she wouldn't give, herself, for one good whiff of fresh country air! It'd be so much nicer to live with Papa on his farm in Kansas, if he were only there.

She didn't think he was, though. Here it was another year, 1888, and Papa still wandered around the country grieving for Mama. And she and Gram were still stuck in Kansas City. How long could she stand it? Feeling stifled, Jocey loosened her scarf. Maybe Gram could spend *her* life bent over washtubs doing others' dirty laundry, but she couldn't. *No.*

A gust of wind caught Jocey's loosened muffler and it went flying into the street. She whimpered in sudden alarm; somebody could see! She clapped her hand over her mouth, and with the other hand she hauled at the reins. "Whoa, Nappy. Whoa, now." She leaped from the cart and ran after the flopping muffler. Hardly ever was she off her guard—worrying about Gram and her own future life must have made her careless.

In seconds the toe of Jocey's small scuffed boot pinned down the fringe of the escaping scarf. She grabbed the scarf up and wound it about her head and lower face. Did anyone see? She looked around, trembling, then she climbed back into the cart and grabbed the reins. "It's all right, Nappy, we can go."

But it was not all right, she saw in the next moment. From behind the houses and picket fences, she spotted them coming. Yelling like banshees, ready for her like always. More than a half-dozen boys and girls. She knew the names of some of them from school, but she didn't go to school often enough to know all of them. Instead, she had one name for the whole group, "The Chasers."

Like a slew of alley cats wanting to kill, The Chasers poured into the street after her. Jocey's throat dried. She steeled herself, hating them for making her feel like a scared rat. A girl yelped, "There she is! There's the looney!"

Hot, angry tears sprang to Jocey's eyes. She snapped the reins across Nappy's back, hard. She didn't like hurting him, but what choice did she have? "Go, Nap! Please. Let's get away from them. Faster, Nappy!" With an effort, the old horse swung into a trot. "Good boy," she cooed to him.

The Chasers nearly surrounding her cart, now, chanted:

> *"Harelip*
> *Ugly Crip*
> *Hole in her lip*
> *Snip, snip!"*

The words ate into her soul like the stones the children sometimes threw bit into her flesh. If only she could pay them no mind. As she jounced along, Jocey's free hand stole up to feel her mouth under the scarf. The top lip separated just off center, since birth. An ugly upside down vee running up into her nose. She knew it was ugly. Although it had been ages since she'd held a looking glass, she knew. She never looked at her reflection in a store window, either, for fear she would break the glass.

Did The Chasers have to keep reminding her she was dreadful to look at? Jocey could feel the warmth of fury rising to her face, then her anger turned to bleeding hurt. Why? she wondered. Why? Why? Why?

Maybe, she decided, if she showed them she agreed with them, playing fun, they would let her be. It was worth a try. She reached behind her and tumbled soiled laundry from a willow basket. She turned the basket upside down over her head and drove on, viewing the street through wickery green. The Chasers screamed with awful laughter.

"Told you she's crazy," a boy's voice shouted. "Ought to be locked up, throw away the key!" There was a chorus of yelling agreement.

Jocey fought an urge to shout back at them, as she rolled along, that she had as good sense as the smartest among them. It wouldn't do any good, though. From the time she was small she had been aware of this odd belief: that since her face was marred, and because she sometimes bumbled her speech from not having a normal top lip, her mind couldn't be right, either. She could prove she was right in the head if given a chance. But The Chasers never gave that chance; they seemed to need a goat to pick on. There was no way to show them who she was, what she was really like. She was so sick and tired of it all. She'd give anything to run—run far away.

Jocey could hear hands clawing at the back of her cart as a chaser tried to hitch a ride. The boy's voice tormented, so close:

> *"Tingle, tingle*
> *Jocey Belle.*
> *Crazy ding-a-ling*
> *Jo—seee!"*

From the blackness at the bottom of her heart— from fear, pain, and frustration—she started a holler that became of howl of rage, a challenge, "Catch me! Catch me if you want to so bad. If you can!" She leaped to her feet in the cart and screamed, "Go, Nappy! Go Napoleon, go!" Given a small miracle, maybe Nappy could outrun them. Oh, she wished it so. Nappy lifted his head as though he understood. The cart lunged as his clumsy canter swung into a full gallop, sending Jocey back hard on the seat. The book thumped to the floor by her feet. Small mud balls thrown up by Nappy's hooves smacked her. She laughed out loud as they flew along, feeling better now, after the release of the scream.

"Good Nappy," she said, her heart full, "you know the way. Soon we'll be home."

Close at hand, as she moved from one block to the next, Jocey could hear an occasional surprised outcry as a pedestrian spotted her flying by in the horse-drawn cart, the basket over her head. She giggled. Unable to stop herself, she swung her fist into the air like an ancient Roman charging to battle.

They might lock her up, though, if she acted this way. More quiet now, she sat down, then took the basket off her head as they neared home.

Soberly, she regarded the row of little frame houses on her block, each one as dreary as the next. The gray rented shack she shared with Gram had been her home for six years, since Mama died. From her reading, she knew there were far finer ways to live. It was getting harder all the time to be content.

In the small, tumbledown stable behind the house, Jocey unhitched. She rubbed Nappy down and gave him grain and water. For a moment she leaned her head against his shoulder. "Rest good, Nappy." She sighed. "We got another day just like this one coming up day after tomorrow, when this wash is done. And then next time, and the next . . ." All her days.

Jocey shook her head, half-ashamed. Gram had stayed on her feet at the tubs as long as a body could, and longer. But now the grippe Grandma suffered got worse and worse. The old soul was bedfast with bronchitis, weak and worn out from coughing.

It couldn't be helped that she, Jocey, must carry on, doing the laundry work alone. As Gram would say, "There's no use fighting the bit."

With her shoulders thrown back, Jocey was ready to go in when her banty chickens, Opal and Don Juan, came clucking to her from their corner of the stable. "Poor little lovers." She knelt and stroked their bright feathers. Every spring the two tried to hatch a clutch of eggs but had no success. Preying dogs and huge rats got at the eggs. It was a wonder Opal and Don Juan themselves continued to outsmart their predators.

Only a pure fool would try to be a farm girl in the city, she decided. Maybe The Chasers weren't so wrong, thinking she was batty. Yet, her tiny garden, Nappy, and Opal and Don Juan gave her more pleasure than any other thing except books. "What would you two think?" she whispered to the chickens, "if I took you to a real farm to live? And you got to raise a batch of fuzzy little babies any time you wanted?" If she could only get Gram to the farm some way . . .

It would be healthier for Gram on the farm, and she could get better. Why did they wait year after year for Papa to come for them? Only the heavens knew where he was, or why he didn't come back to Kansas City. She and Gram ought to strike out for themselves. Go to the farm in Kansas. Not wait any longer!

Contemplating such a move dizzied Jocey. But going to the farm was an enchanting idea, too, and it fastened to stay in her mind and heart. Maybe they could go there, if she could get Grandma well enough to travel. Humming under her breath, Jocey set to unloading the cart. She lugged the full baskets to the enclosed back porch where she thumped them into place by Gram's tubs. The noise caused a thin voice within the house to ask, "Th-that you, Jo—eee?"

"It's me, Grandma Letty. I'm home." Suddenly remembering, she added, "Mrs. Fleck sent you a vanilla custard, Gram. She, and all the rest of your customers, said to tell you they're offering prayers for you to get better soon." From inside, Gram's soft grumble of protest discounted any prospect that she might get better. Why her grandmother persisted in believing she was at death's door, Jocey didn't know. There wasn't a particle of truth to it—Jocey had made sure of that, talking to Gram's doctor. Gram was sick, but she was far from dying.

She ran back to the cart in the stable and found the small covered bowl, Gram's vanilla custard, right where she had jammed it, under the seat, next to the heavy grain box. Luckily it wasn't spilled from her wild ride. She hurried with it into the house.

Gram's form seemed hardly more than a rumple under the patched quilt in her bed near the kitchen stove, where it was warmest. "Feeling any better today, Gram?" Jocey asked. Her eyes smiled down into the faded ones, in a face that resembled crumpled paper. The old woman's mouth pursed dolefully by way of answer.

Giving Gram's shoulder a pat, Jocey went to the stove and stirred the coals. She put in a few sticks of kindling and then chunks of coal. "There," she said, "I'll have us some supper in no time. Gram," she said over her shoulder, "I've been thinking about ways to get you well."

As if on cue, Gram's hard, hacking cough began. When she was finished, she said in a wasted voice, "Hear that?"

"I heard, Gram." Jocey took the tea kettle out to the porch pump to fill. When she returned, she told her grandmother, "I was over near Genessee Street today. Got a new customer. Mrs. John Hanslovan."

"Good!" Gram cackled. Her knobby hands, purplish from years of harsh soap and hot water, were folded over her chest. "If only I can go to my reward knowing you'll never want or starve. It'll be so, as long as you keep up my laundry business I built for the two of us."

Someday soon she had to tell Gram she couldn't carry on her washerwoman business. That not for anything would she put up with the torment from The Chasers for the rest of her life. There had been too many days like today already. As for Gram, her reward—Jocey sighed as she unbuttoned her coat, "Gram, you'll live another thirty or forty years."

Grandma, watching, flinched only a little when Jocey undid her scarf, revealing her face. Jocey pretended not to see it. Gram was mostly used to it, so she never looked sickened, the way others did who were seeing Jocey's face for the first time.

But what did Gram honestly think? Jocey hesitated, putting a check on her feelings first, then she asked, "Grandma Letty—Grandma—am I really a monster to look at? Am I truly bad ugly?"

"No sucha thing," Gram retorted, struggling to lift her head. "'Course you ain't a ugly monster. You would know that for yourself if you'd let us keep a looking glass in the house. Smashing 'em that time just on account of something a little boy said to you at school." She snorted. "Why, if we had a mirror, you'd know you got your mama Kathleen's smokey violet eyes. My Kathleen was a beauty, and you favor her plenty. And you got your Papa Jim's dark curly hair. A girl hadn't ought to be vain, asking for more."

Jocey's feeling of pleasure from the flattery was shortlived. Vain, was she? Gram would do more than break mirrors if somebody laughed continually at her and called her Frankenstein's daughter. Gram would break heads! Was it so wrong to want such things as touching, caring, and laughing with another person? Things she could never have?

"What about my mouth, Grandma?" she asked, intending not to move a step until Gram answered that.

The old woman responded by turning her head away, closing her own mouth and eyes tightly.

That's what I thought, ran through Jocey's mind. She swallowed back aching tears as she went to hang her coat on a peg behind the door. So be it. She must live with her handicap. But *how*?

From the bed, Gram's voice came in a harsh whisper, "Your mouth is my fault, Joee. A hex. A jinx on account of me. But it don't do no good to talk about it. Not good for you, and not good for me, neither."

Jocey whirled back. "What hex, Grandma, what do you mean?"

Whatever Gram's reply, it was drowned in a sudden fit of coughing. Afterward, she lay spent. Jocey asked gently, "Tell me? What jinx, Gram?"

Not that she believed any such thing caused her harelip. Papa once explained to her that it was simply a flaw of nature and nobody's fault. They were all just glad she was whole and healthy otherwise, Papa'd said. Jocey had told him that she understood, and it was all right. But sometimes—sometimes it was hard to excuse God for this foible, this face she was supposed to live with forever. Still curious to know about Gram's strange belief, she asked again, "Grandma, please tell me about the jinx?"

CHAPTER 2

Gram ignored Jocey's question. "I'm awful sick," she moaned. Then, she suddenly changed the subject, "Nobody tried to short you when you collected today?"

It was plain that Gram wasn't going to be pushed, so Jocey gave up trying to find out about the hex for the present. She was glad, herself, to change the subject. Except Gram was into talk about her funeral now, and Jocey didn't like that much better.

"—intend to go out in style," Gram was saying. "It'll take a lot of money. I want a tall gravestone, mind you, Joee. I worked hard and sacrificed all my life an' I think I deserve a real showy funeral. Don't you think so?"

"Yes, Gram, but you aren't—"

"I want my gravestone to be all scallopy on top. I want it to say—LETITIA STERN AT REST. Like that, 'cause for the first time in my life, I will be."

At rest—for the first time *in her life*? Jocey smothered a giggle of horror. "Oh, Gram, let's don't talk about funerals anymore tonight, please? In the morning," she told her grandmother, "as soon as I get the wash on the lines, I'm going to the pharmacy for more of your medicine. Gram, I've got plans, and I'm going to get you well!" She bustled about the small room, peeling two more carrots and another potato to add to the soup bubbling now on the back of the stove.

"No," Gram said with a sigh in a few minutes. "No, you'll never see me on my feet ary again. But you'll do fine after I'm gone." From the tone of her voice Gram could have been expiring that very second. "Do the laundry how I taught you, don't forget nothing. Always add that extra bluing to the rinse water, or extra starch. Them touches keeps customers happy."

Rebellion boiled in Jocey, and she shoved a chair out of her way. Although she held her tongue, her mind was busy. Something she'd maybe inherited from Mama and Papa made her feel she could be, must be, more than a Kansas City washerwoman drudging away her life. She might be a writer, when she got older, or an artist who made pictures for books. There were several possibilities. The lip, *only* the lip, would make it harder. Jocey brought the back of her hand across her nose, for she had started to cry. Somehow she'd find a way around the difficulty; she had to.

Gram was dozing and the soup not yet ready. So Jocey saw a chance to read for a while. She went out to the cart and retrieved her book. With a frown, she brushed a small lump of mud from the blue cloth cover. Her love for books was another legacy from Mama and Papa.

Inside, Jocey drew a chair up close to the stove. Caught in remembering Mama and Papa, she didn't open the book right away. Theirs was a nice love story, the way Papa told it. He was a schoolteacher in his second year when he and Mama met at the downtown library. Mama was only sixteen, a frail girl. She couldn't go to the library often, so Jim Royal started bringing her books. They fell in love. After a while they married. About a year later, in 1876, she was born. *Jocelyn Belle Royal.* Such a pretty name—to give to a baby not pretty at all.

Jocey pushed that thought aside. When she was about four years old, Papa decided he'd had enough of being a simple schoolteacher. He wanted a lot for his family. Hearing about a large gold strike in South Dakota, Papa went there, alone. He didn't find gold, himself, but in a year or so he earned a tidy sum selling hardware to the other miners. And he bought the Kansas farm.

A heaviness settled in Jocey's chest as she recalled what happened next. She got up and gave the soup a stir and then sagged back into the chair. Papa was alone on the farm, getting it ready for them, when Mama died quietly one night in her sleep, here in Kansas City.

Nobody took Mama's passing harder than Papa did. He talked of selling the farm, but he didn't. He took to wandering, aimlessly. He came home twice to Kansas City the year Jocey was seven. When she was eight years old, he returned again, and once the year she was nine. But for two long years now, there had been no visits, and no letters.

It was hard to know what was wrong. She couldn't help but wonder if his staying away was her fault, somehow. The times that he had come home when she was little, Papa had brought her books, and he had played with her, calling her his little "bunny-mouth." It seemed as if he loved her, but maybe, deep down inside, he minded plenty how she looked. Didn't want to be around her. A letter he'd written almost three years ago had come from far out west. Maybe he had a new life, a new family, out there, and was happy without her and Gram.

Jocey stumbled as she got to her feet to set the table, and she came near to cutting her finger as she sliced bread for herself and Gram. Then dipping the scalding soup into bowls, she burned her thumb. Hot tears stung her eyes. "Blast the soup!" she cried.

"The last of the soup?" Gram asked, waking up. "You ate it all?"

"No, Gram, there's plenty."

"Oh." She was relieved. "By the way, Joee, did I tell you we got a letter today? Mr. Porter from next door took it from the postman for us and brought it in. I got sleepy and plumb forgot till this minute—"

"A letter?" Jocey mumbled. She snatched her thumb down from her mouth. "What letter? Is it from Papa? Where is it?"

"Over there by the sweet-tater plant you're growing, on the little table under the window," Gram told her.

The relief and joy spreading through Jocey was intense. Of course the letter was from Papa! She'd been thinking about him and the farm all day. She raced to grab the letter, saw the return address, and her heart sank. It was not from Papa, then. "The letter is from a lawyer, Gram. It comes from Council Grove, Kansas." She tore the letter open and began to read, a frown creasing her brow.

"What's it about? Is Jim Royal dead or something? What's the letter say? Read it to me, Joee," Gram begged.

"There's an awful lot of lawyerish gobbledegook here, but maybe I can explain it." She looked at her grandmother and drew a deep breath, "Some folks out there want to buy Papa's farm. But they don't know where he is to deal with him. Papa's been back only a few times since—since Mama's funeral. They got into the locked house to look for an address to write to and found out about *us* here in Kansas City. They want to know where Papa is."

Gram stared back at her, her chin sagging, mouth open. "But we ain't got no address for him, neither!" she exclaimed in a moment. Behind her curled fist the old woman coughed. "W-write to 'em," she gasped, "say that Jim Royal may be dead for all we know. Joee, tell the lawyer man to go ahead and sell that farm. He can send the money to us."

Jocey was shocked. "But, Gram, we can't do that."

"Don't know why we can't!"

"Because I think I'd know—in my heart—if Papa were dead. I don't think he is. He's alive somewhere, and the farm still belongs to him. And to—to me."

"What do you mean, you?"

She shook the letter. "These people found a deed in Papa's papers. Papa had Mama's name taken off of the paper after she died, and . . . Papa put my name on with his." A quiet joy at this sign Papa cared filled Jocey's heart. "The farm is mine in two ways, Grandma Letty, the way it looks to me. Right now my name is on the deed in trust. And when

Papa dies the farm becomes mine. The lawyer," she added, "says that you are the executor."

Gram looked scared and she puffed up with sudden protest, "I ain't never killed nobody in my entire life!"

What in the world was Gram talking about? Jocey wondered, then she knew. "They named you executor, Grandma, not executioner." She kept her face straight. "I think that means till I'm older, if anything happens to Papa, you are the one to see to it that things go right with his property, according to his will."

"Oh, that's it!" Gram looked sheepish, but her wrinkled face brightened. "Then I say we sell." Jocey shook her head, and Gram fussed, "It is wrong, near criminal, by gorry, for a good farm to lay idle that away for years and not be worked."

Jocey nodded slowly, thinking. "I know, Gram," she murmured aloud; then she repeated with conviction, "I know." Here it was, further reason to head out for the farm, to make a new life there. The farm was not for sale, that's what she would write to the lawyer. She'd tell him that, as Papa's family, she and Gram meant to move onto the farm, in the *near future!*

Gram's figuring was totally otherwise, Jocey realized, beginning to listen to her. "Think of the money we'd get if we sold the farm," Gram was saying excitedly. "You could buy one of them newfangled washing machines that does the work for you. New hot irons, too. Think of me, Joee," she said. "Money like that would mean bushels and bushels of lilies 'roun' my corpse. An' a handsome undertaker in a fine cutaway suit saying glorious words over me, an'—"

"No funeral, Gram," Jocey dared to interrupt. "No hot irons, and no washing machine. Let's go to live on the farm ourselves," she said quickly. "Doctor Hayes says you aren't dying, Gram; but you won't get any better, either, as long as you spend time in the wet and cold, doing laundry, hanging out clothes in freezing air, living in this drafty shack by the smoky old yards. You need good fruit and vegetables and fresh air like on the farm. With that, and your medicine, you could get well. I know. There was a lot about that in my physiology book at school."

"Oh?" Gram's eyes flashed angrily. "Oh, but you're acting high and mighty, Miss. Books. School!" She spat the words. "That's all I hear from you. You like it so much, why didn't you stay in school?"

For a minute, Jocey couldn't answer. Gram's question had gone deep, uncovering her most fervent, unfulfilled wish—to go regularly to school. Finally, she could answer, "Except for the teasing I got, I did like school. Gram, because of my—because I am different, it's always hard. And—and there is no way I can go to school as long as you're sick, remember? I have to take care of you, and the laundry . . ."

Grandma looked guilty, but she still said, peevishly, "Well, you're not doin' such a good job. Where's my supper? I'm hungry."

"I'm sorry, Grandma Letty! The letter almost made me forget about supper." It was good to hear Gram say she was hungry. Jocey put their disagreement out of her mind. She helped her grandmother to sit up in bed. Maybe she could talk Gram into having a second helping of soup tonight, and extra bread and butter. She needed her strength back, if they were going to Kansas.

As though she could read Jocey's mind, Gram said, "You are set to go to that farm, ain't you?" She took three spoonsful of soup in rapid succession. "You'd take me against my will? Kickin' and screechin', you'd still haul me there?" Tiny torches of fire burned in her eyes.

Jocey only shrugged. "Why are you so against going, Grandma?"

"Because it ain't a thing for a near-dead woman to be doing!"

As patient as possible, Jocey said, "I told you we are going to get you better. Stronger, before we go. And we'll wait for the weather to warm up a bit, too." Excitement crept into her voice, "We'll go in the cart. Nappy can get us there just fine."

Gram looked belligerent, but she seemed to lack further words of argument, then.

As Jocey went about her work in the days that followed, sorting laundry, carrying it out to the tubs to wash, and later, bringing clean dried clothes in from the lines to fold, she often caught her grandmother watching her. At times, Gram looked worried. Other times she looked sly and satisfied, as though she was sure Jocey had given up the idea of going to the farm.

Jocey didn't fuss with Gram, but she went right ahead with her plans. Her first bold step was to write to the lawyer to say she and Gram were coming, to stay. Then she found a geography book with a section on the Midwest. There were maps and descriptions of the land. She would use the book for her guide, she decided. Perusing it, she saw that it was only about a hundred miles to Morris County, Kansas. She did her figuring. If they traveled say fifteen to twenty miles each day, they could be on the Kansas farm in a week, ten days at the most. Gram ought to be able to stand a trip no longer than that. Of course they would stop each night and camp so Gram could eat well and sleep lots. She didn't want the journey to make Grandma worse.

Traveling would be fun, and once they got to the farm, everything would be better. Out there, with pure air and homegrown food, Gram's health would improve. And on a farm away from other people, *she,* Jocey, could live free and not worry about folks reacting to her handicap all the time. It would be a godsend for both her and Gram!

There wasn't any question, they had to do it.

If Gram noticed that she was being showered with attention more special than ever, she didn't remark on it. Jocey plied her with tea and chicken broth in between regular meals. She splurged and bought lemons and made hot lemonade as a healthy treat for Gram. While laundry boiled clean in a copper tub on the stove, she sang or read to Gram to put her to sleep for long naps. And it seemed to Jocey that her grandmother did indeed cough less and not so hard. Her color got better.

Gram woke from a nap one afternoon to catch Jocey poring over the geography book, her finger tracing the route they would take, to the farm in the Neosho River Valley.

"What's that you say?" Gram mumbled sleepily. "No show what?"

Jocey realized she'd been reading aloud. She laughed. "Didn't mean to wake you, Grandma Letty." She stilled her creaking rocker and said with caution, "Neosho River, Gram. I was reading about the Neosho River country in Kansas. That's where our farm is."

"I thought you'd come to your senses, girl,"

Grandma wailed. "I thought you'd put that foolishness out of your mind."

"It's not foolish and how could I?" Jocey shook her head and stood up. "How could I forget when it's the best thing in the world for both of us?" Knowing too well she was inviting an explosion from Gram, Jocey gathered her courage and told her that she'd written to the lawyer and told him the farm was not for sale. "I feel that I am responsible for us now, Gram," she finished, "and I can't see anything better for us to do."

Fury showed in Gram's eyes and in the tight set of her mouth. All by herself she slid up into a sitting position. Jocey saw it and was glad for this sign that her grandmother was stronger. "If I ain't heard all! You got no right to make such judgments without my say so. I ain't dead yet, you know!"

Jocey's heart thumped, but she kept her chin up. "Gram, I can take you to the farm. Everything will be just fine."

"Ain't no way atall it could work." Gram shook her head.

Unable to suppress the excitement and confidence she was feeling, Jocey sat down on the edge of Gram's cot and told her, "If a body can read, they can do anything, Grandma." She held up the geography book. "We'll be traveling a main road, Grandma Letty. It's the old Santa Fe Trail; a famous road that freighters used to take goods from here to

Santa Fe, New Mexico. This book has maps. There will be signs. I know the way, the towns, almost by heart." She began to tick them off on her fingers: "Olathe, Gardner, Baldwin City . . ."

Gram looked slightly impressed, but she argued, "We'd die of starvation on the way. Outlaws would cut our throats in the night."

"Oh, Gram, it's not like we're going out west to Oregon. Or crossing the ocean for pity sake."

Gram looked down at the buttons on her nightgown. She traced her chin with her fingertips. "You think you can get us there, to this farm of Jim's?"

"I can. I know I can."

"Awright, say by some miracle we get there in one piece, what then?" She looked up. "You ain't never laid eyes on a real farm, Joee. All you know is what you read in books and from your puttering around in the patch out back. That ain't farming."

"I know that." Jocey got to her feet again, pacing, feeling near to explosion with feeling. "But you know what to do, Gram, and you can tell me." She thumped her chest. "You can tell me," she repeated. "You know farming. I've heard you say how hard you worked on the farm where you grew up, in south Missouri. Isn't that right?"

Grandma Letty nodded. She punched her pillow, and her voice came bitter. "Oh, yeah, I know all about plantin', harvestin', and keeping critters! I know it's back-breakin' work, sunup to sundown. I know a worn-out old woman on her death bed and her girl grandchild who's got feathers for brains can't make a go of it."

"Grandma," Jocey said desperately, "I want to go to the farm for me, too." Her hands clasped the book to her body; she rubbed hard at the knuckles of her left hand while trying to find the right words. "If I have to go through life with my mouth—this way," she whispered, "I'd rather be where there aren't so many people to look at me. I'm so—so surrounded, here. I go out to make deliveries, and I get made fun of, chased, stared at. Gram, do you know that I get reminded every day of my life that I—that I'm a freak? It wouldn't be that way in the country. Most of the time we would be alone, far from other folks and—" she broke off.

A lengthy silence followed. Finally, Gram said, "I got to remind you again, child, life in the country ain't easy."

Jocey found her grandmother's eyes, "The way we live here in Kansas City isn't exactly a play party, Gram. Please, let's go out there to the farm?"

Grandma sighed deeply. "I never thought I'd be lettin' a child take over, tell me what to do. But then, I ain't well. I cain't fight it. All right, all right, Joee, we'll do what you want. See if you can get me there. But—" Her pointing finger halted Jocey's yelp of glee. "I'll likely die along the way and show you who is right."

CHAPTER 3

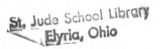Jocey was stacking fresh laundry into a basket the day Gram said tearfully, "I hadn't ought to be going away from here. For nearly forty years I've lived hereabouts. I got to know my customers. I done their clothes, baby garments to funeral garb. A few times there's been layoffs at the meat packing plants and folks couldn't pay me, but I always got by. And they counted on me."

"Gram, you worked so hard—" She wanted to make leaving as easy as possible for her grandmother. "You need a rest. On the farm you can be a lady of leisure, a Queen of Sheba. I'll do the hard work."

Gram seemed to be envisioning that. "I suppose,"

she said finally. Still later, she asked, "Do you know who Mary Jordan is, Joee?"

"Sure." She pictured the dilapidated hovel on Eighteenth Street where the widowed black woman lived with her eight children. Mary, like Gram, was a livestock-district laundress. "I know who Mary is."

"As long as we're leaving, anyhow, I want Mary Jordan to have all our customers. The whole route, from beyond Union Station and all the way past the German Hospital on the hill. You tell her for me, Joee."

"I will, Gram, and I'm sure she'll be glad for it."

Passing the word to Mary Jordan that Gram's wash customers were now hers, signaled definitely that they were going to go to the farm, Jocey felt.

In the next few weeks, a stream of well-wishers—Gram's many customers from over the years—began to call to say goodbye. In past times when visitors came, Jocey would have taken a book and hidden in a corner. Now she was glad the visitors were there to entertain Gram, for she had much to do.

She spent the hours of Mrs. Fleck's visit in the stable transforming a packing crate from the grocer's into a comfy home for her chickens.

On another occasion when a visitor came, she sleeked Nappy for the journey, currying much of his old winter coat into a dark pile of hair on the stable floor. "Do you know how much I'm counting on you for this journey?" she asked the horse. She scratched his head and neck. Nappy shifted his feet and snuffled softly at her ear. She giggled, "You're our steed, and the cart is our chariot, taking us to a magic kingdom."

Jocey sobered. Lacking now, and for good, was the Prince Charming. She lay her cheek lovingly against Nappy, thinking that few humans had ever abided her ugliness this close to them. Animals, it seemed, cared only about the person behind the face. How the person spoke and acted, which was simply a reflection of how a body thought and felt. Humans, on the other hand, attached an awful lot of importance to the face—nice face, nice person. Marred face, awful person. It was an unfair way to judge.

Jocey sighed in an attempt to make the ache in her throat go away. She stroked Nappy a moment longer. She'd never had a truly close friend, boy or girl. There was small chance she ever would. On the other hand, she was going to this new place, and a person couldn't know . . . Oh! No use to dream too big, she told herself abruptly. She went to the cart and jiggled the boxlike structure hard. Noting the shakier spots, Jocey got a hammer and a handful of square nails and went to work to make it sturdier.

The weather warmed as April approached. Jocey could hardly wait to be gone. She sorted their few possessions and listed the most needed ones, which they would take: quilts, Gram's medicines, matches, food for them, and grain for her chickens and Nappy. She decided that there would more than likely be utensils and tools on the farm already; they wouldn't need to take those.

By April first, they were all ready to go, except for one last trip she must make downtown for supplies. Jocey purposefully waited until an hour she knew The Chasers would be inside at school. These days were too happy for her to let the likes of them spoil things.

Pulling on her coat, she asked Gram, "Can I have a bit of your funeral money, in case I need it?" Gram looked so well these days, Jocey felt right in asking. And she worried that the funds she'd put together from their laundry earnings were melting much too fast.

The old woman gripped the side of her mattress where the money sock was hidden, as though Jocey had asked not for money but for her very life. "What if I died tonight?" Gram said in horror. "What then? Me, dead as a doornail and not a penny of buryin' money in the house!"

Jocey opened her mouth to protest, then seeing that an argument would be hopeless, she instead kept silent and took out her list again. She sat down with it and scratched eggs from the list as a beginning. Once in a while Opal took a notion to lay a small nugget, but she might not be inclined to lay eggs at all while they were on the move. She drew a line through the cracked corn for the chickens and subtracted some of the oats she'd planned to buy for Nappy. She had a small amount of grain she could take. Otherwise, the poor things would have to forage as much as they could along the way. Gram's medicines they had to have.

When she'd done all she could with the list, Jocey set out. Bent and well-covered, she threaded her anonymous way through the bustling mid-city crowd. There was a faint taint in the air from the stockyards. Later in the day, when the sun warmed the city, it would get worse.

The druggist at the pharmacy could not hear well and asked her to repeat her order. Jocey pulled her scarf down and with practiced skill she rested her chin in her hand and kept her fingers laced over her sorry mouth while she spoke louder, "Some Blatz Malt-Vivine, please."

"All right," the druggist nodded off-handedly, "it'll only take a minute."

On the sidewalk again, Jocey made her way among barrels and display tables and wished for a lot more money. She didn't have it though. After much deliberation, she decided on a quarter pound of butter and a packet of dried figs to have as special treats for Grandma Letty on the trip.

Finally, she had spent all she could spare. She saw by the clock above the door of the Dollar Hat Shop that the afternoon was passing fast. At home there were last items to be packed into the cart if they were to get off in the early morning as she hoped. Jocey's steps quickened as she headed homeward.

She reached her own neighborhood, and as she passed Maple School, which she had attended occasionally over the years, a keen longing swept through her. It was a sorry, guilty thing with her that she had not gone to school more. She wanted so much to learn. Now she and Gram were leaving. She would keep on teaching herself from old books, but it was nowhere near like real school.

Jocey stood holding her packages, looking up at the parade of tiny kites pasted on the fourth floor windows and at the daffodils on others. With all her heart she belonged here, this was her school, too! Why couldn't they have let her come and be treated like everyone else? Being mocked and taunted had made her feel so stripped of any human importance.

If she had laughed at the abuse, those times she was tripped in the hall or slammed in a door and called a lunatic, would it have been different? When her teachers looked aside, pink-faced, when answering her questions, should she have said something like, "You don't have to look at my mouth, Miss Gant, if it bothers you so. You can look into my eyes. My Gram says my eyes are—fine."

Hadn't she done the best she could to act brave, knowing that to show her true feelings would court further abuse? It must not have been enough. A shrill whistle split the afternoon quiet, and Jocey started. The school doors burst open and hordes of softly chattering, tittering youngsters poured into the schoolyard. Only seconds before the yard had been so quiet, vacant.

Now, Jocey recognized the dark-suited man as Mr. Finley, the principal. Although her feet were taking steps backward, Jocey's soul moved forth toward him, willing the principal to see her and ask her to return to school. But he didn't, he didn't notice her at all. He strode about, checking wavering lines of children. He halted once to speak to another teacher and to look at the pocket watch he drew from his vest. Fire drill, of course. Almost immediately, the students began to file back inside.

Jocey turned away, but not soon enough. One of the few larger boys still outside snickered loudly and yelled out, "Hey, there's the looney! There's old harelip over there." Even from this far away, she could detect the scornful look on his face.

Jocey's vision blurred then, and she ran. Curse them all! She hoped their old school burned down and all the books and everything! Come the blessed morning, she'd be on her way to the faraway farm, and she'd be free.

At home, Jocey stubbornly refused to let the afternoon's unpleasantness stick in her mind. Instead, she gave her full attention to stowing the last of their bundles into the waiting cart. After supper, she caught Opal and Don Juan and put them in the cage she had nailed to the back of the cart. Last of all, she wiped clean the cart's canopy top and made sure all the hooks were securely fastened.

She seldom used the canopy, but in case it rained she didn't want Gram catching her death. She squinted at the cart a moment, thinking that, if you pretended some, it looked like one of those fancy two-wheeled hacks that whirled around downtown Kansas City. No, she decided, not quite.

Later in bed, Jocey had trouble sleeping. She lay awake with her hands folded behind her head. After a long while, she spoke softly into the dark, "Dear Lord, be with us on our journey to the farm. Favor me and Gram all you can, please. We are nobodies down here on earth: me, Gram, Nappy, and Opal and Don Juan, and we're alone. We would take it kindly if you would ease our way as much as possible."

"Amen," echoed from Gram's cot.

Jocey smiled. After a while she drifted off to sleep.

In the morning, she settled Gram in a chair, took the bedding from the old woman's cot, and made a cozy nest for her in the cart. Outside, a pink glow in the east told of a fair day to come, though the air was still chilly. She dressed Grandma Letty in a heavy coat and swathed her head in scarves. The old woman leaned heavily against her later as they made their way out to the cart. Nappy stamped his hooves and shook his head with impatience.

Jocey felt an identical eagerness to be on their way. She locked the doors of the little shanty and then ran next door to leave the key with Mr. Porter, the landlord. "Now, Gram," she said breathlessly on her return, "we can go." Although Gram didn't reply, Jocey could see both fear and high interest in her grandmother's expression.

Under her own muffler, Jocey smiled nervously and climbed onto the seat in front. She lifted the reins, and Napoleon obediently headed out into the street. They were on their way! Really and truly, hard as it was to believe.

At the back of the cart, Opal and Don Juan clucked in soft alarm as they rolled along. Far down the street the bell on a milk wagon tinkled. Nearly breathless with anticipation, Jocey looked back and saw Gram with her head lifted, peering about. "It's wonderful to be out of the house, isn't it, Grandma Letty?"

Gram appeared too preoccupied with gawking to answer. Jocey was glad, until it came to her that her grandmother was telling the old neighborhood good-bye. She swallowed away an itching that started in her throat and lifted her shoulders. No need to be sorry. They were doing right. Everything would be better from now on.

Jocey began to sing under her breath, softly. In

the next hour, as they moved along, they watched the city stir to life. At intersections along the way, other vehicles joined the two-way flow of horse and buggy traffic into and away from the city. Jocey drove carefully, keeping her eyes open and her senses alert.

Every so often she looked toward the far south-west horizon, beginning to dream. In her mind's eye she saw butterflies flitting about in a vegetable garden under a green tree loaded with red apples, a hive of honeybees, and a cow moving slowly toward a red barn. Milk and honey, she told herself, we're heading for a life of milk and honey.

Gram finally broke the silence she'd maintained since they left home. "Glad that ain't us!" she said with a chuckle.

Jocey looked and saw at the side of the road a stalled box-wagon with a broken shaft. The mule hitched to it was firmly planted on its haunches while the driver raged back and forth. "We don't have to worry about anything like that," she agreed with Gram. "Nap is slow, but he's steady, and he's never stubborn or mean."

Soon after, Jocey conferred with her geography book and knew they had crossed the line into Kansas. She told Gram excitedly, "We're not in Missouri anymore! Kansas City is on the state line; we've been in Kansas for maybe half an hour. How does it feel to be in our new home state?"

When she got no answer, not even a disgruntled one, Jocey looked back over her shoulder. Gram was nestled down, sleeping peacefully like a baby in a rocking cradle. Good, Jocey thought. The more Gram slept, the better this trip would be for her.

Jocey's spirits went on climbing as they left the city behind, traveling onward through gently rolling farmland. It suited her that there were few travelers on this road. As a matter of fact, she decided, nothing would satisfy her more than to find that their new home was in country purely desolate. That way, they could be strictly by themselves. A trip to town to trade once in a while, that's all they'd need.

The hours passed, with nought to see but an occasional circling hawk or a farmstead tiny in the distance.

When the sun was high overhead, Jocey and Gram nooned close to a thicket by the side of the road. They ate biscuits leftover from breakfast and one each of Gram's figs. "This is our first picnic, Gram," Jocey pointed out cheerfully, "and we're going to have a whole batch of them."

Gram didn't appear impressed. But she did eat heartily, in spite of her small show of enthusiasm for their surroundings. Later, traveling on, the sun grew warmer. But the old woman stayed under her quilt. "I'm sickly," she stated when Jocey halted the cart to ask if she was too warm, "and sickly stays covered."

Although she worried, Jocey let Gram have her way. Soon, Gram slept. Jocey had little to do but hold the reins while Nappy did the rest. She began to take closer note of the country they traveled. Though they were on a kind of hill, or miles-long swell, they were making good time, she thought.

She'd had no idea, before this, that land could be so flat and monotonous. There were no tall buildings to break the view, like in Kansas City. And there was so much wide blue sky—hundreds of thousands of miles of it! From time to time, Jocey had to shake herself awake in the warm sunshine as Nappy trotted on.

To break her boredom, Jocey gathered a mental picture of a band of screeching Indians and made them rush at them, into the drowsy quiet of the cart. She rubbed her tired eyes. Indians didn't go on the warpath anymore, though. And besides, she'd had The Chasers. She wanted no more of anything like that.

Later in a field to her left, a farmer ceased plowing and waited for a boy crossing the field toward him with a water jug. Jocey watched them as long as she could.

Twilight fell when they were but a few miles short of Olathe, Kansas. For some miles, Jocey had kept watch on a stand of trees ahead in the distance. Now she pulled into them. "We'll stay here tonight, Gram," she called over her shoulder. "Stay covered in the cart till I can kindle us a fire from some leaves, twigs, and whatever I can find." Gram mumbled an answer as Jocey jumped down from the cart.

Jocey felt apprehensive at the newness of their venture, but she didn't want Gram to see it. When the campfire began to snap and glow, she helped Gram to a log she'd rolled close to it. "All right, Gram," she said, her hands clasped in front of her, "how about some hot tea? And supper?"

Gram nodded without speaking. Her grandmother was hardly ever this quiet at home, Jocey thought, worrying. Gram was tired and scared, she reasoned. No doubt as scared as she felt, though she was trying to hide it. With a little more time, they'd both get used to what they were doing. Things wouldn't seem so strange and out of kilter.

Gram looked up into the dark branches above them later, and she rolled her eyes. She held a cup of tea in one shaking hand and a slice of buttered bread in the other. "Kind of scary," she whispered. "It's a fool thing we're a-doing, child. We got no business to be out here alone thisaway."

Jocey drew up to protest, to put on a bluff if she had to, but Gram wasn't finished, "I don't feel very s-safe here, Joee. But at the same time I feel—I feel like this is a kind of adventure, you know? I'm sort of glad I can do a thing like this, one last time. Makes me feel young. Full of courage, real grit, like you."

The confession so surprised Jocey she was speechless for a moment. Her relief poured out in a long sigh. Why, if Gram went on feeling like this, it was going to be a big, big help. "Gram," she said confidently, "any troubles that get in our way are going to be little ones." She handed her grandmother a second slice of bread wrapped around a sizzling strip of fried pork when the old woman made her wants known with a motion. Jocey finished in a smaller voice, "Any big troubles come our way, we'll just lick them, too!"

She felt much more relaxed as she tackled her own meal, not talking. Later, she had to admit the quiet of their surroundings bothered her some. She wouldn't have guessed she would miss the heavier, harsher sounds of the city, but she did. Far away, now, a farm dog barked. Close at hand, small creatures, nameless to her, skittered in the brush.

Well, it was *different,* that was all. As things would be, from now on. Different didn't have to be bad. Different could be good.

CHAPTER 4

"Joee, I cain't sit up no more," Gram said, when she'd finished her second cup of tea. "Help me to my bed in the cart. I'm awful tired. For a while tonight, I thought I was glad I come. But right now I'd near give my soul to be at home in my own bed."

"I'm sorry you can't be, Gram, but we'll make you as cozy as we can. You'll see. This isn't forever. We'll be at the farm in no time. Please don't worry about anything. I'm going to roll up in my blankets on the ground, right next to the cart. There, see—" This was only their first night. They had to keep heart, both of them. "N-nobody, nothing, will bother us, I know. This good night air will help us sleep good, and it will be morning before either of us knows it. We can be on our way again, and everything will be just fine."

"I don't know, I don't know. Anyways, quit your preaching," Gram said, sagging against Jocey as she helped her toward the cart.

Next morning, Jocey woke cold and cramped, hearing her grandmother's hacking cough just above her. Gram couldn't be worse! She'd been doing so well before they left Kansas City. Jocey got out of her blankets and hurried to build a fire. With water from their jug, she stirred up a pot of bubbling oatmeal. Her scalp was tight with worry as she worked, and from time to time she looked at Gram in the cart, who'd fallen back to sleep without eating. They wouldn't have to turn around and go back, would they?

She squatted and stared at the popping oatmeal bubbles, trying to think. They really didn't have so far to go if they went ahead. In just days they would be there. And they would be passing through several towns along the way. If Gram got bad, they could stop in a town for help. And if worst came to worst, she would get a room for them and hire out to do housework to pay for it—hiding the fact of her mouth some way. As soon as Gram got better, they could go on again. They wouldn't need to turn back.

Jocey's worry went deeper when Gram refused

breakfast, wanting to stay in her bed in the cart, sleeping. Giving up, finally, Jocey gulped her own food, packed their things back into the foodbox, and got them onto the road once more.

As they drove through the town of Olathe, Jocey looked about with anxious curiosity. It was a busy place. Several teams with farm wagons were hitched at the rails about the town square. A group of men, farmers and fine-suited businessmen, stood talking on the courthouse steps in the morning sunshine. They took no note of her and Gram passing by, and Jocey was relieved.

The nice homes and stately elms made her half-wish they were stopping here themselves, for good. But no, Gram was not really complaining yet, and their farm waited. An honest-to-goodness *farm*. Not a postage-stamp sized radish and onion patch, with a run-down shed, in the crowded city. That was not for her, not anymore.

Two or three hours later, they stopped by a creek to make tea. "Feeling better, Gram?" Jocey asked, after she'd coaxed her to take a dose of cough syrup. Her grandmother nodded and wiped her quivering lips on the back of her hand. "How about a little exercise?" Jocey asked her, then.

Gram shook her head. "Leave an old woman be, Joee. I'm just confarnal tired." Molelike, she burrowed back into her blankets.

Jocey smiled to herself. If Gram's only problem

was tiredness, she needn't worry so much. And Gram did seem perkier later that afternoon.

Now and then they approached other travelers; horsebackers, or a wagon or buggy. Wanting to be un-noticed, Jocey scrunched down into her collar and stared straight ahead. But Gram, always the more sociable one, sometimes called out in greeting.

That second night, Jocey lay half-awake, stirring nervously each time her grandmother made a sound. If Gram did get worse, if she—*died*—on the way like she'd said she might, it would be her fault alone.

What would a person do with a—a body, 'way out here like this? How could she have the fine funeral for her that Gram had always wanted? Jocey's heart began to pound furiously. Worst of all, what would she do all alone, without even Gram for company?

Twice in the night Jocey scrambled from her bedroll to get Gram a drink of water and a spoonful of medicine. The coughing let up, but still Jocey lay awake. She was up at first light.

When Gram finally stirred, Jocey had had a fire going for some time and she had eaten her own breakfast. "Are you all right, Grandma Letty? How do you feel?" She didn't want to, but if Gram was worse they could still turn around and go back to Kansas City.

Gram's eyes batted a few times, and she yawned. She seemed to fall asleep again, and Jocey waited.

Finally, her grandmother growled, "I ain't dead yet. That's something." A hint of a grin touched her withered lips, and her eyes opened. "You were the one who told me I couldn't die. Wasn't going to for a long time. Now, on this trip, you act like ary breath I take is my next to last one. Joee, ain't a germ got a chance in this old body the way you keep dosin' me!"

Relief filled Jocey to the point where she felt she couldn't breath. There was thankfulness in her breathless laugh. "All right, Grandma! Not so much medicine if you think I am pushing too much at you. But we aren't giving up on healthy food and lots to drink. I wish the farms weren't so far off the road, I'd like to buy three or four eggs and some milk. I'll see what I can do in some town today."

Bread and tea wasn't enough to keep their strength up. Besides, if they ran out of money, at least there was Gram's funeral savings they could turn to. She'd seen Gram stuff the fat old sock into her coat pocket before they left Kansas City. She just hoped they wouldn't have to fight about the money. Gram's agreeing to come on this journey to the farm didn't mean she had relinquished her dream of a fancy funeral, that was for sure.

Jocey kept the geography book on the cart seat beside her with reason. North of Gardner she showed Gram a landmark, an old signpost. "To the right it says 'Road To Oregon,' see, Gram? Pointing left it's marked, *'Road To Santa Fe.'* Lots of pioneers traveled this way before us. Doesn't it make you feel good, going right along the same road, on the very ground they traveled? 'Course, they had a lot farther to go than we do."

"Didn't know I was coming on this trip for a history lesson," Gram admonished. But then, and still later, she seemed to enjoy the stories Jocey told her about the landmarks they passed.

Heartened herself, about almost everything, Jocey slept sound the third night of the trip. She arose full of energy. Unneeded energy in the cart behind the plodding Napoleon. Would she never get used to the tedium? Jocey wondered as the hours wore on. Beyond Baldwin City, later in the day, the scenery finally changed. Dingy shacks and dark mounds marked small coal mines on either side of the road. Jocey found the sight interesting but decided she much preferred the farmsteads and grazing sheep, which they also saw.

That day seemed to pass more quickly, and on the fifth morning she felt like giving a loud cheer. If her guess was close, they were now well beyond the halfway mark. Half the journey over!

Her happy mood changed late that afternoon when Nappy began to limp. "Whoa!" Jocey drew up the reins, and she hopped from the cart before its wheels ceased rolling.

"What's the matter?" Gram yelped. "Why we

stoppin'? Are outlaws holding us up?" Her head came out of her bed like a turtle's, to look.

Jocey went back to her. "It's Napoleon." She sighed. "He's thrown a shoe from his right front hoof. We better find a blacksmith. I'm going to walk so he won't have such a load to pull. Burlingame is somewhere up ahead. Maybe we can get there before dark." Or not. Maybe dark would find her stranded alone beside the road with a sick grandmother and an injured horse.

Their progress had been slow before, but now they seemed to crawl by half-inches. Jocey walked at Nappy's head, on and on, endlessly. They were a few miles short of Burlingame when night descended. So be it, she thought, since there was no way to alter the situation, anyhow. She hadn't ought to've pushed Nappy this far, probably. They'd make camp, all get a good night's rest, and head into Burlingame in the morning.

She didn't like to deal in towns, though she'd had to for fresh milk and eggs, but this was an emergency. Nappy had to be shod. Besides, she had a whole bag of fancy tricks to keep her mouth hid from gaping, nosy strangers, if she needed them.

Gram seemed much better, that was one good thing. She paced a few toddling steps while Jocey roasted potatoes in the coals of their fire and fried a few strips of salt pork in a skillet. Every now and then, Gram hesitated next to Jocey, kneeling by the fire. Finally, she blurted, "You ought to quit hiding it, Joee."

"Hiding what, Gram?" Jocey asked innocently. Could Grandma read in her eyes the dread she was feeling about town tomorrow?

"You know what I'm speaking of, child. Your mouth. I can see you're not wanting to face folks, to have Napoleon shod in the morning. Written all over you." She scolded, "As long as nothing can't be done about it no way, you ought to stop hiding, as though you don't have no harelip." Her voice gentled. "You ain't foolin' nobody but yourself, Joee."

The flames of the campfire blurred before Jocey's eyes. What could Gram, what could anyone really know about it? She spoke through an aching throat. "People *don't like* to see my mouth, Gram. That's why I don't show it. And I don't appreciate being thought ugly. Nobody would." She stood up, changing the subject in a broken voice. "I have to get our pl-plates from the food box so we can eat." In the shadows by the cart she turned, "Don't worry about me, Grandma Letty. I'm all right. I can manage." She'd found her answer—to hide away from the rest of the world on Papa's farm. If the world didn't want her the way she was, she could get along without the world. Period.

On their way next day, Grandma again set to urging Jocey to "just be your own sweet self." That was much easier said than done. But Gram would consider it "sass" if she said so aloud, so Jocey remained silent. Gram's nagging, though, began to get on her nerves. Just in time, when they entered Burlingame, the old woman fell silent.

A morning southwind stirred the trees that lined the broad main street. It was a rambling town with comfortable-looking houses. Once again Jocey yearned to be settled in their own place. But she could wait; only a day or two more and they'd be there.

In the meantime, she rather admired their reflection thrown back by the long deep windows in the limestone shops, her and Gram rolling along in the cart behind Nappy. She was reminded again, with some pride, that they were travelers west on the Santa Fe Trail.

After a bit of seeking, Jocey found a livery stable and blacksmith shop on a side street. She halted Nappy beside a pile of old horseshoes and other scrap iron and got down from the cart. A husky man worked just inside the huge barn. Her pulse hammered in her throat as she went to speak to him. All the while she was aware that Gram watched from the cart.

Because he was pounding a horseshoe at the anvil, the man didn't hear her request the first time. "I need my horse shod," she practically shouted, then.

The indifferent look he turned on her made Jocey feel knee-high and unimportant. "Too busy," he muttered. "If you want to leave your horse, I may get around to it tomorrow."

Tomorrow? He *may* do it tomorrow? They had to get on to the farm; they couldn't be held up that long.

"There will be a feed bill, too, for stabling your animal," the smith said, then he went back to his pounding.

Jocey spoke loudly from behind her muffler, "We are just passing through this hour. Couldn't you shoe my horse now, please?"

He wiped at the beads of sweat on his brow, and his glance took in the heavy muffler she wore with suspicion. It was a warm morning. She suppressed a nervous urge to giggle. Maybe he thought they were on the run, hiding from someone. "You alone?" he asked, and Jocey felt her stomach lurch. "No man with you?" He looked toward the cart where Gram hunkered, waiting, her eyes as wide and inquisitive as an owl's. "Well," he sighed, "if you got cash money to pay me, I'll do it. It'll be tw— fifty cents."

Jocey dug into her pocket for the coins to show him. He nodded, and she hurried back to Gram. "He's going to shoe Nappy for us," she said as she unhitched her horse. She knew the blacksmith was taking advantage of them, doubling his price because they were just an old woman and a strange-looking girl, alone. If he paid no mind to her face, she reasoned, and if he shod Nappy quick so they could go on, it was worth it to her. "While we're waiting, let's go sit over there." She pointed to a tree a few yards away.

Within minutes, she was spreading a blanket on the ground and cushioning a quilt for Gram to sit on. While the blacksmith worked on Nappy, inside by the forge, she and Gram ate a late, cold breakfast.

After Burlingame, the road turned south for a few hours before it angled due west again. Jocey knew a sense of well-being as they traveled. Even after several days on the road, Gram didn't seem any the worse for being out on the road instead of in an invalid's bed. She had taken to sniffing out sights of interest, herself, and she called Jocey's attention to them.

CHAPTER 5

"Look at that oriole settin' on the cattail yonder, Joee," her grandmother called out one time. "Fool bird thinks it's real spring. Bet he wishes he'd a stayed south a whist longer."

Jocey looked and smiled. At the same time she took note of Gram, who had her quilt up under her chin. The old woman's nose was pink. Gram, being old, must feel the cold more. Regardless, she decided, this fresh air was better for them than the stockyard rot.

A while later Gram asked, "Ever notice how chimney smoke looks like people and such, Joee? See, over there is a fat clown over that farmhouse way yonder." She pointed across the treeless prairie to the distant farmstead. "An' there," she yelped, "is a skinny scarecrow thinnin' up outta that one."

Delighted to join Gram's game, Jocey laughed and said, "I see it, and there's a curvy damsel coming up from that farmhouse chimney up ahead there."

"Damsel, smamsel." Gram snorted, behind her. "That's a fish smoking a pipe as sure as you were born." She added sympathetically, "Afraid you ain't got the eye, Joee."

Unmindful of the criticism, Jocey smiled, content that Gram was in good spirits. Napoleon seemed to have caught their mood, also, and he stepped as lively with his new shoe as an emperor leading an army. At the back of the cart in their crate, Opal and Don Juan cooed like contented love birds.

Thus the sixth day of their journey passed. That night they camped beside a small, tree-lined stream. Jocey found it—the Marais des Cygnes River, which she thought was pronounced, "Mara Da Zeen"—on her map. "Gram, listen to this!" she said, after she'd read about the river in her geography book, following supper. Good smells of the potatoes they'd fried and campfire smoke hung in the air. "This says—" She held the book close to her face because the campfire light helped little.

Before she could go on, Gram interrupted sleepily

from her pallet in the cart, "I was near to noddin' off. I don't want to hear nothing from a book this time of night!"

"Gram, please. You know who Evangeline was, don't you?"

"The painted woman from that saloon down by the stockyards in Kansas City?"

"Heavens no, Grandma! Evangeline is the sad heroine of Henry Longfellow's poem. She was in this country, according to the story, Gram. She and her friends came down the Great Lakes, after the British ordered them out of Acadia. She'd gotten separated from Gabriel, her sweetheart, and she was very unhappy. With her companions, she followed the Illinois River, then the Mississippi. They came up the Missouri River to here, right here! This river used to be called the Osage."

"Sounds to me like she was a fool, lost," Gram grunted. "Which we may be too, as far as that goes."

"No, Gram, Evangeline wasn't lost, not really. She and her French friends were looking for a place to settle, and the Osage Indians guided them here. In the village that was near here, Evangeline heard a story about a princess named Osa, who was loved by a young war chief of a hostile tribe. His name was Coman."

"Do I have to listen to this?"

"Please, Gram, you'll love it. Now, Osa's father didn't want her to marry Coman. He even said he would kill the young war chief if he didn't stay away."

In the shadows, Gram leaned forward, her eyes glistening now with curiosity. "Did the pa take a hatchet to the young feller?"

"Wait, Gram. Here's what happened: One time Coman came to visit Osa, after he'd been ordered not to. Her tribe ran after him and chased him to his canoe. As Coman was leaving by the river, which was flooded at the time, Osa jumped into his canoe with him. She couldn't bear to be separated from him, see. Anyway"—Jocey swallowed—"they paddled hard out into the middle of the awful flood waters trying to get away."

"An' did they?"

"No, Gram, their canoe upset and they—sank from sight. Osa's father and the others in her tribe felt just awful then and sorry for what they'd caused. But it was too late. While they looked, two beautiful white swans came up from the waters where the canoe upset; they swam away t-together." Jocey sniffled. "Together."

"Did the saloon girl, Evangeline, drown and turn into a swan, too?"

"No, Gram," Jocey groaned, "please don't get mixed-up. This is a beautiful story, don't spoil it."

"Well, I can't help it," Gram stormed. "People running crazy all over God's country and turning into swans."

Jocey persisted, "Please. Listen, now. After Evangeline heard the sad tale about Osa and Coman, she went wandering into the woods and up a hill. Maybe —maybe right over there." She pointed at a knoll looming purplish in the gloom. "At the time, Evangeline was grieving for her own lost lover, Gabriel, remember? From the top of the hill, Evangeline looked out on the green valley with the shimmering stream winding through the marshlands. Everything looked so beautiful to her. She spread her arms and said, *"C'est le marais des cygnes!"* Jocey drew a deep breath, *"This is the marsh of the swans."* A feeling of awe had enveloped her. It was as if time had rolled back, and *she* was the courageous Evangeline, making the proclamation.

After a brief silence, in a voice soft and husky, Jocey added, "That's how come her French friends always called the Osage River the *Marais des Cygnes,* Mara da Zeen." Jocey began to recite from memory the story poem, *Evangeline:*

> *"This is the forest primeval. The murmuring*
>   *pines and the hemlocks,*
> *Bearded with moss and in garments green,*
>   *indistinct in the twilight . . ."*

When she finished, Gram spoke thoughtfully, "I need a bath and I thought to take me one in this here river tomorry. But I ain't takin' a chance a' turning into one of them swans." She looked toward the river and the surrounding darkness as though she were searching for the ghosts of Evangeline, the Indians, and the Frenchmen. "It was a pretty story, Joee," she admitted, "but I got to caution you. Your nose is in books a terrible lot, and I wonder is it good for you?"

Jocey laughed suddenly, and she circled her arms about the geography book, holding it close to her breast. "I'll always be glad Mama and Papa taught me to read when I was tiny. And that Papa brings me books when he comes home to visit. *When* he comes. Gram, I can be anybody I want to be, do anything I want to do, or go anywhere I want to go— just in reading a book. Isn't that fine? Take China; I'll probably never get to go there, but I can read all about China and that's almost as good."

After a few minutes, with a stick, she raked the scattered coals of their fire into a small glowing heap. Above them, the wind made a lullabye in the trees. Her throat filled achingly, and she whispered, "I wonder where Papa is tonight?"

"In that Chinee, likely!" Gram exclaimed. "With his head in some book same as you. Joee, don't count on seeing your Papa again. If he's got the itchy-foot I think he has, he may never come back." She sighed. "It's time we got to sleep. I declare you've wore me out with your yammering."

In the night Jocey dreamed about Papa. Something was wrong. Papa tried to reach out to her but dim figures caught him and pulled him back. The tortured look on Papa's face as he called her name, brought Jocey up, screaming aloud, "Papa! Papa, what's wrong?"

"You're havin' a nightmare, Joee!" From the cart, Gram's voice cut through the awful dread that held Jocey and brought her full awake. "Go back to sleep now. You'll have the whole countryside down on us, screaming thataway!"

She slid deeper into her blankets, shivering. Only a nightmare, but so real. Jocey tried to go back to sleep and couldn't. She'd never thought before that Papa might want to come home but couldn't. What if that were true? She'd thought first it was his grieving for Mama, and later, the shame of having her as his child that kept him away.

She slept fitfully into the night. Once she woke to find herself free of her blankets, lying on the bare cold ground, crying, "Papa." Sniffling, she crawled back to her bedroll and rolled into its warmth, like a cocoon. She was determined not to let the bad dream come back.

She slept again, and when she woke next, it was from the feel of wet lizards' tails rasping across her closed eyelids. Another dream, she thought, brushing at the imaginary lizards. Her hand connected with something soft and furry!

Jocey's eyes jerked open, and she stared up into

the face of a large bewhiskered yellow dog. As he tried again to lick her face, she ducked her head under her blanket, mumbling, "G'way! Get!" The sound of human footsteps approaching set her heart to racing even faster. Jocey peeked out and saw overalled legs, heavy work shoes, and a gun barrel. They were going to be killed. She shivered from a sudden intense cold.

If only they hadn't overslept. Now, Gram, too, was awake. She yelped, "Don't shoot, mister. It's just me, here, and my little grandbaby girl. Whatever 'tis, we didn't do it. We're innercent."

Keeping the blanket about her face, Jocey dared to sit up slowly. "What do you want?" she said behind it, as bravely as she could manage. "We're doing no harm. Let us be." Her muffled voice disquieted the yellow hound dog. He whined and ran sniffing around her as though to determine what kind of animal she was. Jocey drew away.

"Quiet, Thor," the man finally spoke. "Calm down, boy."

Jocey didn't detect anything threatening to them in the stranger's voice, but it was too quick to make guesses. Her glance traveled suspiciously up the overalled legs to the bib, the coat collar, and into a hickory brown face and gray eyes smiling quizzically down on her.

He pushed his battered gray hat back on his head. "I do apologize if I scared you," he said, turning his gun aside and resting the muzzle on a rock. "I came out this morning looking for Posie, our milk cow who is going to calve any day. I saw your horse and cart over here. Can't tell what kind of fiddle-foot, no-good outlaws might be hanging around, so I went back for my gun and come to see."

"You can see we aren't outlaws," Jocey mumbled, pushing the yellow dog away from her for the third or fourth time. " 'Bye."

"Yup." The farmer appeared amused, "I can see you ain't outlaws, and I best be on my way." He started off. Then he turned to ask, his tone serious, "You ladies been travelin' far, alone? Have you got far to go?"

Jocey wished he'd mind his own business and just leave.

Gram spoke in a rush, "We come from Kansas City. I ain't well. But this hardheaded girl is set on our gettin' to her papa's farm here in Kansas—only he ain't there. Ain't seen him for a couple years, and . . ."

Mention of Papa reminded Jocey of her bad dream, and a cloud seemed to darken the morning. "Gram," she protested, her face hot, "that's our affair, not this man's." Gram knew better than to tell a perfect stranger her whole history, didn't she?

But in the cart, Gram was sitting up, patting the wild gray haystack of her hair into place. She smiled. "Mister, is your house close by?"

"Gram," Jocey warned.

"Across the road and down the lane," he said. "Say, you two come have breakfast with Emily and me. My wife sets the finest table in Lyon county. Emily loves visitors. I recall her mentioning hotcakes and ham." He motioned. "How about it?"

Jocey's mouth watered, her empty stomach churned at the thought of such good food. But of course they couldn't go with him, and Gram shouldn't have wrangled the invitation. Her handicap was only part of the reason. She was sure if they made good time today, they could be on Papa's farm, their own place, by nightfall. Home, their home!

"We have to be going. But thank you, anyway, Mister," she mumbled. She waited, wishing he would go, so she could get up and wash and dress. She supposed she ought to be glad he'd come by though, and that his old yellow dog had roused her.

"Hotcakes and ham?" Gram was saying. "Oh, my." She went on, sounding embarrassed for Jocey, "We can't hurt this kind feller's feelings. Country folk is always neighborly to wayfarin' strangers. You don't know that, Joee, growing up in the city like you did. Now why can't we go along with him? Come help me get ready."

Didn't Gram realize that this farmer wouldn't have invited them in the first place if he had seen her face? Maybe Gram could forget so easy, but she couldn't. Even if he was the rare sort too kind to take back his invitation once he got a look at her, she still couldn't go. His wife, his children if he had any, wouldn't be able to hide their repulsion, and *she* couldn't bear their ogling or their looking away.

"We—we just can't go with you for breakfast," Jocey said in a low voice. "We—we don't have the time. Gram, quick as I can get our things together, we got to be going." A frown wrinkled her forehead, and her eyes narrowed. The farmer seemed to catch her meaning, that he must go before she could come out of her blankets. He turned and snapped his fingers to the yellow dog that had lain down near Jocey.

Gram spoke quickly, to hold him, "My grandchild is a mean bossy girl as you can see. It's crazy, dragging me off to this Kansas farm. But tell that to a know-it-all girl." The man kept going. Gram's voice rose, "She thinks it is going to be a storybook adventure on her Pa's farm, a picnic in the meadow every day. Sir," she yelped, motioning him back, "you're a farmer. You know how 'tis. Tell Joee, here, that farming is work."

Jocey glared at Gram, but it did little good.

The farmer's sober look seemed to take effort as he called back, "Farming is work, young'un, your grandmother is right enough about that."

Gram snorted her triumph, but Jocey wasn't swayed and she didn't reply.

The farmer went on, "If that is what you are set to do, I admire you, young lady. But I doubt very much a little girl and an old wom—you and your grandmother, can make a go of it, with no menfolk." He shook his head. "Like my own Pa used to say, 'you got to be up before the lark' every day, and—"

"He's speaking of birds," Gram interrupted, "meadowlarks. An' they get up mighty early in the mornin', a'singing and workin'."

The pair of them had her itching with anger. She didn't have all day to argue, but she could tell this farmer a thing or two he might not know—about Genessee Street. The stockyards where every hour you could hear the animals scream from death blows. Where the carcasses and blood and lard-melting planks stank up the neighborhood so bad you wished you didn't have to breathe. And the long aching hours bent over hot soapy tubs wearing your knuckles thin on other folks' dirty clothes! By comparison, most anything would be paradise. Even for a "looney" harelipped girl.

"I'm waiting for you to go so I can get up!" The belligerence in Jocey's voice surprised even her, and Gram looked ready to pop. The farmer hurried off, the yellow dog trotting after. "I'm sorry, Gram," she said, her anger cooling, "but we'll get to the farm sooner, now, and you'll be glad. Today, Grandma."

"You ought to be whupped." Gram gave her a stony, disbelieving look. "If I wasn't so weak and near to dyin', I'd do it, too!"

Jocey tried to explain, over their quick breakfast

of dried figs, a hunk of bread, and milk. "Gram, you can see for yourself that eating is the one thing I can't do and keep my face covered. That farmer was nice. For you, I wish we could have gone for breakfast at his house. But he and his folks wouldn't want my face at their table to look at, I just know. I'm real sorry, Gram."

Her grandmother didn't answer. Jocey's guilt deepened as they continued on their way. It was awful what she'd done to Grandma Letty, because of her stupid handicap. Gram loved people; chatting with her customers was the thing Gram loved most about being a washerwoman. Breakfast with the farmer and his family would have been such a treat for her; maybe she should have let Gram go alone.

For the next several hours Gram remained withdrawn, not speaking nor smiling, until Jocey was close to tears from feeling responsible. Come noon, her Grandmother would not eat. Jocey's pleading fell on deaf ears. Gram had never been so stubborn, so angry with her as this, before. Or was part of it that Gram was getting bad sick again? Since Gram refused to say either way, Jocey was at a loss what to do.

It came to her with a feeling of surprise, later, that they had covered a considerable distance since the meeting with the farmer. She'd been so preoccupied with Gram, the miles had gone by unnoticed. The end of their journey must be only a few hours away!

She pushed aside her feelings of worry and guilt over Gram's hurt and told her cheerfully, "That little town of one street that we passed through a while back was Allen. Gram, that means we only got nine more miles to go. Aren't you getting anxious to get there? I sure am!"

It bothered Jocey little when Gram didn't answer this time. More important now, they were nearing *home*. She got out the lawyer's letter, which gave the location of the farm. Coming up next was a town named Bushong, she noted. Only six more miles to their place! She sat up straighter, her heart nearly filling her throat. She viewed her new world as though she were seeing heaven. And it was beautiful.

New green showed everywhere in this Neosho River Valley. In farflung pastures, herds of cattle and horses grazed peacefully. Tiny farmsteads, marked by turning windmills, were spaced miles apart. Really *miles!* As she had expected, as she had hoped!

An hour or so later, Jocey said over her shoulder, "Going to put you to bed as soon as we get th-home. You'll be warmer inside shelter, and you won't have to be bounced along like this ever again, Grandma."

"Thank the Lord," Gram mumbled, breaking her silence at last. She began to cough, a sharp, genuine bark that scared Jocey. After a while, Grandma Letty spoke again, "Good farmland like this here would sell for a pretty penny. We should of sold Jim

Royal's place an' stayed put where we was. That's what we should a' done."

Jocey heard the forlorn disappointment in Gram's voice. But her own rising spirits couldn't be checked, sorry though she felt for Gram. She asked breathlessly, "Are you looking, Gram? Isn't it fine? We're going to be there soon." She wanted to add, *"You won't be sorry. The farm is going to bring us a pretty penny from what we grow on it."* Not willing to risk riling Gram again, she left the remark unsaid.

After a while, Jocey picked up the lawyer's letter once more, and she examined the map sketch closely. When she lowered the paper to her lap, her mouth was dry and her heart beat furiously. They had reached their own property line, beginning just about—*here,* this stone fence.

For a moment, Jocey could do nothing. Then, with a shaking finger she pointed to a toy-sized cabin and outbuildings outlined against the deep blue sky. "G-Gram, the—the house over there. See it? That is our place." She snapped the reins, "C'mon, Nappy. Old sir, there's your new home."

CHAPTER 6

"This ain't a bad piece of land," Gram chortled as they creaked along. Her anger at Jocey seemed to have vanished. She went on, "I wonder did Jim Royal get many crops in? Sandy river bottom soil," she said, "is perfect for growing 'taters and watermelons. This'd be fine country for growing garden truck."

Jocey turned and nodded in delight. *Potatoes, watermelon*—she rolled the words silently off her tongue. That's what she would do, then. She would find out from Gram how to go about planting "garden truck" and be at it right away. This summer they would sell what they couldn't eat and preserve. Likely they'd make a good living.

Her eyes burned as she stared at the little cabin and outbuildings growing larger and larger. She'd been watching the road a long while and she had strained her eyes, or was it her happy feelings spilling over? She blinked several times and kept looking.

The fringe of trees behind the farmstead must line the creek, she thought. Fox Creek, her creek.

"Joee, you can't take the whole road," Gram squawked suddenly. "Let these folks by!"

She broke from her reverie, realizing that there'd been the rattle of wheels behind them for some time. But she'd paid little heed. Now, Jocey guided Nappy toward the shoulder of the dirt road and stole a look at the wagon rattling by.

A stern-looking man drove the team; a plump woman beside him smiled hesitantly at her and Gram, who waved. Several flaxen-haired children were stuffed into the wagon behind the couple. They stared, and spoke to one another in a garbled tongue Jocey couldn't make out. From a foreign country, they must be. Scandinavians, likely.

With a frown, Jocey watched them move on down the road. She hoped they lived quite a ways away. It was her desperate dream that she and Gram should be alone, far from other folks. Not that she had anything against them personal . . .

As she watched, the children turned to stare back at her and Gram. Their voices grew high with excited chatter. Then, the father's voice clapped like thunder. The youngsters quieted instantly.

Jocey dismissed the other travelers from her thoughts as she approached the lane to the farm where they must turn off. She could scarcely breathe from excitement. She wanted to see it all. Every blade of grass and chunk of earth. Every bird and gopher and grasshopper that lived on their land. She held Napoleon to a walk, and the weary old horse seemed grateful.

The house before them was built of up and down boards, bare of paint. There were few windows. She took note of a stone barn in back of the house, along with two smaller outbuildings; and at the end of a path by a sagging clothesline was an outhouse. Out front of the house new grass peeped through the swamp of last year's dead grass. Beside the house, three small trees were covered with swollen leaf buds.

This was Papa's. Jocey moistened her lips and hauled up on the reins, stopping Nappy. Papa'd been here a lot, she guessed, although the place looked much too deserted for him to be here now. She realized that she'd been carrying for some time a deep-down hope that Papa might be here. He wasn't. That was plain to see. She put down an ache of disappointment.

"Let me get you into the house, Gram." She tossed

the reins aside and got down, her own limbs hurting and stiff. "I'll build us a warm fire if there's something to burn. I think I am going to have to get in through a window." There was little daylight left, but as soon as she'd settled Gram, she intended to explore.

Inside, their footsteps rang hollow on the wide dusty boards of the floor. Jocey helped Gram into a horsehair-stuffed chair beside a potbellied stove at the back of the front room. On a peg behind the stove hung a jacket she recognized as Papa's, decorated with spider webs. There were three shelves of books below the east wall. Papa's, of course. Even when their colorful spines were coated with dust, books made the room homier. Jocey wiped her eyes and hurried into the kitchen. A woodbox held a few sticks of wood and lumps of coal. Without further ado she built a fire, and in minutes the empty shell of a house began to warm.

The only other room was a bedroom that contained a large bed, a chair, and a dresser. Jocey opened the door to the room wide so that the heat would flow into it and got Gram into her nightgown. "Where you going to sleep?" Gram whispered when Jocey'd gotten her into bed. Like a tired child, Grandma grasped the corner of the pillow; her eyelids fluttered.

"Until I can fix myself some kind of cot, I'll have to sleep here with you, Gram, in Papa's bed. But don't worry about anything, now. I'll come to bed, later. You go to sleep."

Jocey returned to the kitchen for a closer examination, standing with her hands on her hips. There was a dry sink, a large cooking range, and two cupboards. What more did they need to be happy here? She went to the kitchen window and drew the dusty curtain aside. Outside on a fence post near the barn a bird—maybe a lark, maybe not—fluttered its wings and sang a song to evening.

Why couldn't they make a go of it, be all right, here? Like Gram had said about her, she had the will. She was young and strong. All she'd ever wanted was here. Except for Papa; she'd like him to be here, too. And she wished Gram was in better health. But Gram wasn't going to die, she was more sure of that than ever. Gram was going to get much better. And maybe Papa would come home, too.

Jocey tiptoed into the bedroom and saw that Gram was sleeping.

After she'd heaped their bundles and boxes inside the kitchen door, on the floor, she led Nappy to the musty barn. She put him in a stall and gave him the last of the oats she'd brought with them. Signs of Papa were here, too. A second old coat hung from a peg on the wall, beside harness and rope his hands had no doubt held. Jocey turned quickly away and went to bring Opal and Don Juan into the barn. She turned them loose in the hayloft. One of the extra sheds had turned out to be a chicken house, but for now she felt it best if the chickens and Nappy kept each other company in their new home.

With long confident strides, Jocey left the barn. She stopped at the other shed, a coal shed, and took a basket of fuel along to the house with her. On the enclosed back porch, she filled a bucket from the pump there. A few minutes later, while her last onion, a chunk of salt pork, and potatoes boiled in a rich stew on the stove, Jocey set to work cleaning. Why wait? she thought. She could get a few licks in yet today. With old rags she found in a cubbyhole in the kitchen, and with hot water, she began to wash utensils, the table, chair, and shelves.

She stored their few remaining staples and canned goods. Before long, she knew, she would have to make a trip to town. Why hadn't she thought to ask for some of Gram's funeral money to buy more food and other supplies when they came through Bushong? A person at the head of things needed better sense than that. Well, she had a chance to learn a lot, from now on.

The first few days on the farm, Gram felt too poorly for Jocey to leave her and go to town. A trip to Bushong, even, would take most of a morning by her figuring. In the meantime, Jocey'd found two guns in the house—a handgun with a long barrel and another gun of the sort held to the shoulder.

Rifle, she thought it was called, or maybe shotgun. Whichever, she determined to trade one of the guns for what food supplies and garden seed they needed. Someday she would just have to buy Papa another gun, if he came back.

On the fourth day after their arrival, Jocey knew she had to go to town, or else. They couldn't starve, and they had to get crops into the ground now, for later.

She had found a huge old almanac among Papa's books that told all about seed: how much to order and how and where to plant. There was also doctoring advice for both humans and farm critters, along with recipes for everything from pie to soup. They'd get along. She moved the book to the kitchen where it would be handy.

"I'll be back sometime this afternoon," she told Grandma Letty when she was ready to leave. She tucked the quilt up close under the old woman's sagging chin. "Stay in bed and rest easy while I'm gone."

With a bit of her old fire, Gram retorted, "I—I was plannin' to get up and dance me a Shoo Fly."

Jocey nodded and suppressed a giggle. "You'll be fine, and I'll be back before you know I'm gone." She drove Nappy as fast as he would move, north toward Bushong. Along the way, in green pastures near town, grazing cattle awaited shipment from the railroad depot. They bawled lonesomely as she passed, for lost calves, Jocey supposed. Sometime, she'd like to have a cow for milk, and a few beef cows like these. That would be far in the future, though, when she and Gram—and maybe Papa—were rich.

Bushong was a small, sleepy, country town, and Jocey liked it that way. There were seventy-five residents, according to a boastful sign, and there were only about nine or ten business establishments—so different from Kansas City. Soon, Jocey was heading Nappy toward the one general store.

Inside, she laid her list carefully on the counter and waited for the thin, moustached storekeeper to read it. She murmured behind her muffler, "I'm in special need of seed potatoes, three bushel at least."

"I reckon it's not too late to plant spuds. We'll see what I got left." His glance sized her then. "You are a stranger to me, Miss. That means I got to have cash, you know. Can't give you credit."

Jocey reached inside her coat to bring out the long-barreled handgun. It dipped and shook in her hand. The storekeeper stared a fraction of a second before his hands flew upward, her shopping list fluttering away like a bird. He flung himself backward, almost tipping over a stack of casegoods.

"W-wait, I—I don't mean . . ." Jocey looked down at the gun in her hand. She turned it toward the storekeeper butt first. "I—I only meant to trade the gun, for supplies. The gun was my father's, but he's gone . . ."

"Oh." The storekeeper wiped at his moustache. "Oh." He leaned against the counter. "You really scared me, Miss." He took the gun, then, and studied it for a full minute through squinting eyes. "Not bad. I can let you have twenty dollars, that be all right with you?"

"Will that buy everything on my list? And the garden seed?"

He nodded. "You'll have half the money left over."

"Oh, good! That's more than I thought—I mean, thank you." Unless she could get Gram's burying money away from her, this fund must do them for a long time.

The storekeeper moved about the store, gathering onto the counter the bags of beans, flour, sugar, and can of lard and other items he read from her retrieved list. Jocey moved slowly about a table covered with bolts of cloth.

"Where is your place, Miss?" he asked her after a while.

"Southwest," she mumbled, not looking his way. "About an hour from here."

"You must be neighbor to that Norwegian family, then. Edvard Pladson and his flock. Your folks got a big family?" he asked.

Did he have to be so nosey? Jocey shrugged by way of answer.

"I can hardly hear you, little gal. Got trouble with your throat?"

She touched it and nodded. This busybody would like to keep her talking all day. But she had to get home to Gram. Jocey pretended deep interest in a bolt of green-sprigged dimity. Later, she accepted her change and helped load her goods into the cart, in silence. At last she was urging Nappy back down the rutted road toward the farm.

It seemed to take hours longer, going back. Nappy wouldn't be hurried. Maybe he was afraid they were headed on another long journey and he didn't want any part of it. In spite of the cozy warmth of the afternoon sun, Jocey experienced a sudden chill, as a feeling came to her that ahead on the farm something had happened.

For all she knew, Gram could have pneumonia. What if poor Grandma got to coughing and choked to death while she was all by herself?

The moment she drove in the yard, Jocey scrambled from the cart and ran. On the porch her glance caught some huge dirty footprints—a *man's* shoeprints, not hers or Gram's. Some of them led to the door—and on inside. Her throat constricted. *Gram!* Oh, Gram! She wanted to scream, but couldn't. She raced through the house and into the bedroom.

Gram sat propped up on pillows in the bed. She

was smiling and talking to herself. "—and then I said, 'Beulah, you bring your wash to me and pay me when you can. All them babies, them diapers, why—'" She broke off at sight of Jocey clinging to the doorjamb. "Grandbaby! You're home. Joee, I had a visitor—"

"I know you did! Are you all right? Who was he? What happened?"

"Why are you so fussed? Everything is hunky-dory." Gram smoothed the quilt that covered her thin frame. "He was a peddlar man, Joee, a walkin' peddlar man. Knocked on our door, and I called him to come in."

"Gram—a stranger? You let him in?"

"We had a nice visit, too." Gram nodded. "He was a gentleman and interested in the folks I knew in Kansas City. First good chat I've had since we left there—"

"He might have murdered you in your bed."

Gram hooted and her chin jutted stubbornly. "Nothin' of the sort. Joee, ain't you never going to learn to trust nobody? He showed me his whole pack-ful of gimcracks and stuff. Gave me medicine for my congested chest, a potion made from yarbs and roots like we used to have back home in the hills. Better'n that fancy Kansas City stuff been doin' me no good." From the chair by her bed, she picked up a small brown bottle that Jocey hadn't noticed before now. "I had only a leetle bit, but I feel better, Joee."

She giggled. "I don't think it's all yarbs. I think there's spirits in it, too."

Sozzled? "Oh, Gram—" Jocey found her way to the chair and sagged into it. "I know how lonely you are, but you mustn't ever do anything like this again. I'd hoped we were far enough away from other folks —but I suppose a peddlar will be' coming by now and then, and others, too. Gram, we have a shotgun. I want us to learn how to use it."

"Pshaw, Joee. He was a nice walkin' peddlar man, that's all. I invited him to come again. Sometime when you're home, he'll show you his ribbons and perfumy soaps and all. You'll like him."

Jocey shook her head, unable to scold her grandmother any further. Gram did look better, happier, some way. Partly due to the liquor, no doubt. They would talk about this more, later. Gram thought she was too distrustful. But she had plenty of reason for it; years of torment and ridicule had taught her to be extra careful.

"I have to unhitch Napoleon," she said. "When I come back in, I want you to tell me everything there is to know about planting potatoes." She had the big book to go by, but she didn't want anything to go wrong. She needed all the help she could get.

Whatever was in the medicine the peddlar gave her grandmother had worn off by the time Jocey got back to the house. Or maybe it was the medicine that had put Gram to sleep. The old woman's chin was on her chest, and she snored softly.

After a few more days of "feeling puny," as Gram put it, she seemed better. Jocey was doubly pleased. It was hard to work out of doors for any length of time when she had to stop every so often to go into the house and check on Gram. But there were many times when she had to go indoors anyway, to ask Grandma Letty how something was done.

By the second week, she hated to admit it to herself, let alone to Gram, but getting the farm into operation was going to be a whole lot harder than she'd thought it would be. If climbing out of bed at daybreak each day had been all of it, it would have been easy. But a body could have all the desire in the world, she discovered, and still flounder.

Lying in bed one night, aching from work, Jocey thought back over the troubles and mishaps she'd had since they had come here to the farm. She had cut herself, not once but twice, trying to file a sharp edge on the rusted plow blade. Then there was the morning she found Don Juan, torn and bloody and near death, under the back stoop. She could do nothing but hold him and sob helplessly. It broke her heart all the worse because down in the barn Opal was setting on a clutch of five eggs, her and Don Juan's first family-to-be on the farm.

Gram had taken the near-limp chicken right into bed with her and gently and expertly sewn his wounds with needle and thread. She then doused the incision with the medicine the peddlar had given her. "A fox got your little rooster," Gram told Jocey. "But he'll live if you keep an eye on him. Pen your chickens up tight, child."

When the plow was finally ready, she'd brought a double fistful of dirt into the bedroom to show Gram, as her grandmother had requested. Gram fingered it. "Yup. Dry, friable," she said. "Get on with your plowing."

Jocey had hitched Nappy to the plow, and for hours they made a jagged procession up and down the large field between the barn and the creek, sunup to sundown. The rich, loamy smell of the fresh-turned earth she took as a sign of accomplishment. And she threw away the rags bandaging her hands when there were more blisters than she could cover.

By the end of the fourth day of plowing, Jocey had a large patch of ground broken into crumbles. It looked to her as huge as the play yard at Maple School in Kansas City. She'd helped Gram to the window to see. "I got about two or three acres worked up, ready to plant. That's about how big that plowed parcel is, don't you think so, Gram?"

Her grandmother, looking, snorted. "Child that ain't hardly more than an acre. Your measurin' eye is 'way off. If we're going to earn our keep off that ground, you got to have five to ten times that planted."

"H-how much?" Jocey was stunned.

"Why, at least five acres in garden sass, another five acres just potatoes, and five acres ought to be in corn. If you want to earn anything off it, that is. Some seeds'll come up, some won't. Wild rabbits will get their share, too. Got to take all that into account, you know."

It could have been her imagination, but it seemed to her that Gram had watched her slyly after that, for signs of giving up. Thinking about it now, Jocey turned into her pillow to whisper, "I can do it! I can do it, I can!" Only how could she, how could she get everything done by herself? If Gram would hurry and get lots better . . .

As it was, Gram's only assistance was to give advice. She showed Jocey, for example, how to cut the seed potatoes into quarters, leaving two or three "eyes" to a chunk. "Put 'em under the ground about as deep as your hand, say five inches or so," Gram instructed from her bed. "Two or three chunks to a hill. Come summer, you'll see more taters than you ever dreamed could be."

She wouldn't doubt it. As the days went on, Jocey felt half-dead from the plowing, but finally she had fifteen acres prepared for planting. The potatoes would be their main "money" crop, she decided. She found that planting was child's play compared to getting the ground ready for the seed. It was simply a matter of making a ditch with her hoe, sprinkling in the seed, and covering it over with dirt and tamping the dirt down. Nothing to it.

In the "garden sass" acres she planted lettuce, onions, and radishes. Then carrots, beans, and beets; and cabbage, turnips, and squash. Finally, watermelon and pumpkin. A full five acres was planted to corn, besides the five acres already planted to potatoes.

Jocey couldn't have been prouder. She and Gram would feast like royalty, she thought, when the tiny specks of green began to show above the ground. The garden could produce none too soon. Luckily, for now, there were wild berries and greens to pick down by the creek. Once in a while she caught a fish or two. Their cash, after two more trips to Bushong for food staples, was low.

They needed the garden badly, but she watched in alarm as it came up scraggily, with more weeds than vegetables. Jocey nurtured with care the vegetable plants that came up, and replanted with leftover seed those plants that failed. The weeds were a constant challenge. But the blisters on her hands turned to callouses, and her muscles hardened and gradually she grew accustomed to the long hours of work.

She loved being outside, where with advancing summer the air was heady with the perfume of wild roses. Jocey likened the air to her own life, which she considered rosier, happier, than she'd ever known it to be.

Alone in the house all day, recovering slowly, Gram was not nearly so content. One morning, as Jocey was cleaning up after breakfast, in a hurry to get outside to the weeding in her gardens, she heard Gram yelp from the bedroom, "Stop them! Yahoo those folks in here, Joee, hurry!"

Jocey looked out the window and saw the Norwegian family, the Pladsons, going by in their wagon. She'd seen them driving by more than once in past weeks. In spite of Gram's plea, she didn't move.

"Invite those folks in for coffee and a chat, Joee," Gram yelled again at the top of her lungs. "Joee, you hear me? It's time we meet our neighbors. Get a move on, now, they're gettin' away!"

CHAPTER 7

Except for the few trips she'd had to make to town, Jocey had managed to have the isolation she wanted. She'd come here, after all, to get away from the eyes of other people. No telling what she'd start if she went out now and invited these people in as Gram was begging.

Maybe Gram would think she wasn't in the house and hadn't heard, if she left. Jocey tiptoed across the kitchen floor, stole out the back door, and ran to the barn, her face aflame with guilt. She went through the barn and out to the back pasture. In another minute she whistled through her teeth to Nappy. When he came, she scratched the horse's ears and his long, bony nose. "What am I going to do, Napoleon?" she whispered as he tossed his head and then nuzzled her shoulder. "If my mouth wasn't this way, things would be so different. I'm being mean to Gram, and I hate myself for it."

She stroked his rippling sides a moment longer. He nibbled at her fingers then. Through a choked voice she said, "I've got nothing for you this time, Nappy. I came out of the house in kind of a hurry. But wait till you see the carrots I'm growing for you." She'd better go in and tell Gram she was sorry. But after that, what?

As she neared the house, it came to Jocey what she might do in the future. Best of all, it was something Gram could look forward to, now. A fine idea! Jocey laughed and ran the last few steps to the house.

Inside, she caught Gram out of bed, storming back and forth across the kitchen floor in her bare feet. Gram looked most hale for a body who insisted on having every meal brought to her in bed. Shocked, Jocey sucked in her breath, "Gram, I didn't know you—"

Her grandmother whirled and pointed an accusing finger, "You been makin' a jailbird outta me, and it ain't fair. You got no call to treat me thisaway. I got it in my mind you saw them folks passing by and you didn't lift a finger to hail them in for me. Joee, you ought to be ashamed!"

"I am, Gram, I am sorry, but you—?"

Gram's tirade wasn't over, "This keeps on, I'm

hanging a white flag, a signal for help, out my window. You'll see, girl, how much company that brings!"

"You won't have to do that." She held up a hand to keep Gram still. "Listen, please. I know how lonely you've been, and I know what we can do to change it." Why had Gram hidden the fact that her health was much better? Jocey was side-tracked into wondering. She'd been doing for Gram constantly, running errands, waiting on her hand and foot. On top of all the farmwork she had to do. It must be she'd been too busy to notice that Gram looked downright hearty. She swallowed. "I thought as soon as you're up to it, I might drop you off at church in Council Grove on Sunday mornings. Would you like that, Gram?"

A sudden smile replaced the anger in the old woman's face. "Church? Everybody going, all decked out on Sundays? Oh, yes, Joee, I would like that. But do you think I can ever get that strong again?" Her hand suddenly clawed for the back of a chair, she seemed to sag all at once from her head to her toes.

An act! Seeing Gram's behavior for what it was, beginning to understand, small mysteries began to come clear to Jocey. The extra slice of raisin pie that disappeared; shells from eggs she hadn't boiled. It was Gram, up and around, doing it! How long had this been going on? Why would Gram pretend to be sicker than she was?

Gram *enjoyed* being a loll-a-bed. The more Jocey thought about it, the more unfair it was. How many times lately could she have used Gram's help so desperately? So many little jobs that took so much time. But she'd worked long hours like a dog, alone. "When you're well enough, Gram, I'll take you to church." Her voice came clipped. "It's up to you."

Grandma Letty looked as confused as Jocey'd ever seen her. "Oh, I don't know," she whined and crept into the chair to sit down. "I'd love to go to church sure enough. You think I could? No," she answered herself. Guilt came and went fleetingly in her face. "No, I'm far from well. These things take time. Folks don't get as sick as I been, kissin' old man death almost, and then bounce right back. We'll have to see about it, though, sometime . . ."

"You know best, Gram." Jocey felt like she and Gram had changed places, and she was talking to a child, a naughty child. She couldn't hate Gram for her dishonesty, but neither did she intend to let her get by with it much longer.

Of her own accord, Gram began to sit in a rocker on the porch for a few hours each day. Her eyes followed Jocey at work among the young vegetable plants. As the days grew hot and the soil drier, she came up with an idea for getting more water to the garden than Jocey could pack by the bucketful.

"You better dig some channels from that creek into your tater patch and gardens. Dam the creek about right there," she pointed. "Use rocks and sticks and mud, and whatever you can put your hands on, to stop the flow. Turn that good water down thisaway where you need it."

Jocey decided she could at least be grateful for Gram's knowledge, and she was. That day, and for three days after, she worked building the dam, until she began to smell as fishy as the creek. It was hot, heavy work that muddied her from her head to her feet. But a beaver couldn't have made a better dam, she decided when the wall of stones and sticks was completed.

The morning after the dam was finished, she was back at the creek, busily digging more channels toward her garden, when a laughing voice called from far down the bank, "So that's it! Now I see what happened to all our water."

Jocey's hands flew automatically to her face. Except for the mud, it was uncovered. She took one quick look at the tall blond boy approaching with a fishing pole on his shouder. Not uttering a word to him, she scrambled out of the water and up the bank. Her heart was like frozen ice inside her as she raced away across the field toward the house, to hide.

A boy, a boy about her own age. Blue-eyed, fair-haired, he was one of the Pladsons, Jocey felt sure. It was hard to get his nice, smiling face out of her mind that night, although she tried. Would he have the good sense not to come back? For certain, she hadn't shown him welcome.

Next day, Jocey hoed in the potato patch, wearing Papa's old straw hat pulled low to shade her eyes. The sound of a horse coming from the direction of the willows bordering Fox Creek made her look up, startled. She wanted to run, but the rider's hard stare held her frozen. She gripped the hoe handle. Why couldn't she be left alone?

"My boy come by here yesterday. Told me it was you who dammed the creek," the gaunt-faced man on the black horse uttered, a trace of accent in his voice. "I come see for myself the person who would be so stupid to try and take my vater."

This was Edvard Pladson, then, the father. Jocey kept her chin down, hoping the shadows from her hat hid her face properly. "I—I didn't know the creek ran through your property, too, or anybody else's. I didn't think." She had taken it for granted that the creek was hers, and Gram hadn't said otherwise when she told her to dam it. Of course she couldn't take all the water if others depended on it, too.

"I—I'll tear up the dam," she said in a moment. Her potatoes had gotten a good soaking, the flowers looked fresh on the dull green plants. And she could go back to carrying water by the bucketful if she had to. It wasn't easy, but—

"Why do you just stand there?" Edvard Pladson demanded to know.

She glanced sideways up at him, sitting on his horse, watching her. He—meant *now?*

"I got eighty head of sheep down dere at my place nearly dead from turst. I wait while you tear down the dam."

Sheep dying? She hadn't meant any such thing to happen. Jocey nodded and started for the creek. Mr. Pladson came behind on his horse. Trembling, Jocey waded into the warm water of the creek, and bare-handed, she began to tear loose the rocks and dirt from her dam. All the while, the back of her neck itched from awareness that the man watched, sitting like an ironman in his saddle. She was doing what he wanted. Why didn't he just go away?

After a long while, he asked bluntly, "You are kin to Jim Royal?"

"Do you know my fath—?" she started to turn, forgetting for a moment her face. Excitement lurched within her. "You know Papa?" she asked over her shoulder as she reached for a boulder.

He didn't answer directly. When he did, his voice threatened. "If you are Jim Royal's kin, den I want you to stay away from my family. Don't come sneaking around, trying to ruin them the way he did."

Sneaking? Ruin? What was he talking about? Jocey pulled the boulder away, at last, and wiped the sweat from her forehead. Keeping a muddied hand on her hatbrim to hide her face, she turned toward him. "What about my father? What are you talking about? I want to know."

"Keep away, that's all I say." He reined his horse to go. "And next time you try to dam my water away from me, I go to the law."

If that wouldn't take the skin off a turnip! Jocey watched him ride away, chewing her knuckle, tasting dirt. What a hard, mean man he must be, she thought, snatching her hand down. His wife and children, the nice boy with blue eyes, must have a terrible time of it. And what was this about Papa? Papa'd never do anything to hurt a person; he wasn't like that at all.

On the other hand, this Edvard Pladson appeared to her to be the kind who would hate at the least opportunity. He was nearly out of sight, and her stomach still felt quivery from their clash. She yanked off her hat. With a vengeance, she went back to tearing away the dam, tears running down her cheeks.

Later, a southwind stirred life into the quiet afternoon, lifting her hair, tossing it, cooling her. She was reminded that, no matter what, it was good to be alive. Good to be *here*.

The week wasn't out when Jocey looked up from repairing the barnyard fence to see a tall stooped figure making its way toward her up the lane. "Rains it pours," she muttered, dropping a short pole. If the farm got any busier, it would be like Kansas City.

She squatted down out of sight and watched him come. Too late, she realized that Gram was all alone up at the house and might need her. Pulling her hat low, Jocey raced for the house. When she got there, Gram was out on the back porch, full of smiles, welcoming the stranger as she might her dearest kin. Jocey halted and gasped for breath.

"He's come back, Joee," Gram called to her from the porch step, "the peddlar man I told you about. Remember, the gentleman who gave me the medicine, when you went to town?"

From astonishment more than habit this time, Jocey's hand flew up to cover her mouth. She stared at Gram's gentleman. The walking peddlar was an Indian. There had been Indians around Kansas City, mostly rancher types who came and went with shipments of cattle. They weren't so raggedy as this man, she thought, her glance sliding over him.

A leather strap across his forehead helped hold the heavy pack that rode on his back. Below the strap, coal black eyes peered back at her with a hint of humor in them. There was a deep diagonal scar across his face that squashed his nose in the center, but in spite of it, he appeared likeable and kindly. Of course, that remained to be seen.

"Joee," Gram spouted, "this is Tom. Tom Thunder-Dog, didn't you say your name is? He's a Kaw Indian. Lives on a reservation in Oklahoma when he ain't on the road, peddling." Gram waved him to come in. At the same time she ignored Jocey who stepped forward to stop Gram, frowning in warning.

"This is my grandbaby, Jocey Belle Royal. Looks awful don't she, so dirty and sweaty? She ain't hardly got the time to fix up is the reason. But I want you to show her your ribbons and other pretties."

Feeling helpless, still off guard from surprise at Gram's guest, Jocey followed them with cautious stiffness into the kitchen. Tom Thunder-Dog took off his pack. He turned it up and shook the contents out onto the floor. In spite of herself, Jocey felt her eyes go wide with delight. The Indian squatted beside the pile and held a fistful of ribbons up for her to see.

"Are they pretty?" he asked. His scarred face made her less conscious of her own disfigurement. Jocey smiled at the rainbow of ribbons he held. She couldn't resist kneeling to take a good look at the unbelievable array on the floor. There were wall plaques and egg timers. Needles. Small bundles of cloth in every color. Many spools of thread. Lace. Rings and bracelets. It would take her hours to identify everything.

From the look on Tom Thunder-Dog's face, something was missing. He reached behind him and brought forth his rumpled pack to shake it again. Out rolled pans, a tea kettle, a tiny doll, and a tangle of beads. And—and something else. Jocey reached a hesitant hand to pick up the smashed ladies' hat. It was navy-blue straw with a veil. *A lovely veil.*

She smoothed it into shape. Still kneeling, she took off Papa's hat and put on the other, pulling the cloud of veil down over her face. Her throat tightened, and she stood up and walked to the window, not seeing, but thinking. In this hat she could go to town and not worry about her mouth being noticed. Most of the time when she'd gone out in Kansas City, she had worn the heavy muffler—winter, spring, summer, and fall. She was free of that old scarf now, out here living this new life on the farm. And she didn't want to wear that old scarf to town anymore, either. Her vegetables would be ready to market, soon. In this pretty hat she could call on stores, go to houses door to door. Be herself without worrying.

When she turned, she saw both Grandma Letty and Tom Thunder-Dog watching her. "It is yours, because you are so pretty in it," the peddlar said.

Jocey started to shake her head.

"We can give him dinner to pay for it," Gram said quickly, "and visit a spell."

She was glad her grandmother wanted her to have it, too, but—"Gram, that wouldn't be enough," she whispered.

"I have come very far today and I am tired. Tonight I can sleep in your barn?"

Jocey considered this turn in their dickering. She wanted the hat so desperately. "Yes," she said, "yes."

"Good. But we still not even." Tom Thunder-Dog's coppery fingers combed the goods on the floor. "Here, take this, too." He held a blue velvet ribbon out to Jocey. "This is for you." He gave Gram a string of pink beads. "Now we are even."

At dinner, Jocey couldn't help being interested as Tom Thunder-Dog talked. But she felt sad for him, too. From earliest times, it came out, the Kansa or Kaw people, his people, had been uprooted and made to move from one place to another. Worse, smallpox and liquor introduced by traders had caused the tribe to dwindle until only a few descendants, like himself, survived. "Our last home, before Oklahoma Territory where we are now, was near Council Grove, here in Kansas. I was a boy when we were taken away from here. But I remember this valley. I like to come back."

"Now see," Gram said, after the Indian peddlar had departed next day, promising to stop in again later in the summer, "didn't you have a good time visiting with Mr. Thunder-Dog?"

Jocey had to admit she had. She wished there was some way for her and Gram to have company now and then. Without concern for her stupid face.

There wasn't much time for socializing, anyway, though, she decided. Weekdays, now, Jocey worked long hours under the broiling sun. She picked potato bugs off her plants. She hoed weeds. And endlessly,

endlessly, she carried water by the bucketful to her garden, until she wanted to scream from backache. Instead, with gritting teeth, she began to regard each blister, ache and callous as a medallion earned for a mission completed.

On June seventeenth, Jocey turned thirteen, but she felt much older. The weeks passed into summer. Due to her work, Gram's advice, and more than a few miracles from God, her garden thrived and fed them well. While Gram would not help with any of the picking or the sorting or cleaning of their vegetables, she did happen to be well enough to attend church every Sunday from the middle of June.

On Saturday afternoons, Jocey took her produce to market, her head high under the navy straw and its veil. She took care to arrange her choicest produce colorfully, and she priced it fair. Early on, she'd learned there were two or three other farmers who peddled their produce in the surrounding towns, and she must compete with them. Many townspeople had their own gardens. But several of those who didn't became her steady customers. Coin by coin, their savings began to add up.

She was thinking, on the way home from one such trip to market on a Saturday, that her and Gram's worries were about over. They had a good home, plenty to eat, and there was even a small savings in the sugar bowl in the cupboard. And today she had been able to buy dress goods! A gray chambray for

Gram. Not that it would help her much to be pretty —her thoughts were on the Pladson boy at the time —but for herself she had chosen a print. Heart-shaped green leaves and purple violets on white, the violets to match her eyes.

If only there was an escape from her face, but there wasn't. She was not a girl with a nice, regular face and that was that. She needed to learn, if there was a way, to get along better with the face she had —its flaw and all, she decided. With a lot of trying, maybe she could. She might even someday rise above it to the point that it didn't matter to hardly anybody. And not to herself especially. Such thoughts, new to her, made her feel surprisingly better inside.

She and Gram would be all right this winter, she decided; there was no worry there. She intended to dig a root cellar and store away as many of her vegetables as she could. Come next spring, they would plant again. Things would get better and better. Like the plants, she and Gram had a good foothold on life here and could count themselves lucky for that.

Approaching home, Jocey's eyes eagerly sought out her handiwork, the verdant vegetables that *had* come up and *were* producing, her gardens that made her so proud. What she saw made her scream, "No! Oh," she moaned, "oh, no."

The fence about her potato patch had been mashed down as if it were a spider web. White bubbling backs of sheep filled the green of her garden.

CHAPTER 8

In the yard at last, Jocey came off the cart on the run. A sob caught in her throat. She grabbed a shovel leaning against the back porch and raced at the sheep, shouting, "Get out of here! Go away you stinking things. Get out of my taters, get, shoo!"

She whacked at the ground, whacked at the sheep, her breath coming in tortured sobs, "Get yourselves out of here."

Suddenly, a belled sheep turned away from her threatening shovel and trotted out of the patch. The others fell in behind. Jocey watched through tears as they meandered slowly away in the direction of the Pladson farm. Her aggravation and hurt turned to bitter anger when she saw how many plants had been chopped into bits by the flock's small hooves. And so many vegetables had been eaten, or half-eaten.

Would Mr. Pladson do this intentionally? To get even with her for damming the creek? Surely he wouldn't have! She'd torn the dam down. Calming in a few minutes, she realized that the sheep must simply have gotten out of their own field and wandered this way. Whatever had happened, it had to be the last time! She couldn't go to the Pladsons, not even to complain.

In the kitchen, later, Jocey told Gram about the damage to their crops.

"Do what you can to prop up the stems that's just bent and not broke," Gram advised her. "You can save a lot of 'em that way. There's still taters under the ground they couldn't touch. But the late sweet tater plants will need the stems and leaves to take in sun and water."

Jocey nodded wordlessly, then went out and unloaded the supplies she'd bought in town. She unhitched Nappy, and he shook himself and followed along to the pasture in back of the barn. As he cropped the green grass, Jocey leaned against the gate and told her old horse-friend, "There's so much to do, Nap. If it isn't one thing, it's another, and I don't get any help from Gram."

She had intended to start scything wild hay in the morning, to put up for Nappy, for the winter. Now she would have to do what she could for the plants that the stupid sheep had raided. There was the fence they'd torn down to fix, too. Maybe she could get to work on it right away if Gram would make supper for them.

Gram sighed heavily at the suggestion. Her head sagged toward her shoulder as she spoke, "You make such good biscuits, Joee. Make us some nice ham-gravy and biscuits. And a pot of spinach, and slice some tomaters, too. That'll be good. And I better have my supper in bed."

Why was she doing this? Jocey bit her tongue to keep from snapping out at Gram. Grandma might even have chased the sheep away today and saved all the work she had to do now. She'd had to go into town to sell their garden truck, herself. Gram could have started their supper. By anybody's eyes she was fit enough to do small chores.

When was Gram going to admit that she was well and able to do her fair share? Jocey opened her mouth to voice her ill feeling, then she closed it. She didn't have the heart, the courage, to sass Gram, her elder. All she could do was wait, and hope, a little longer. "Supper will be late. I'm going to see what I can do about those mashed plants. Some of them will be dying already."

Twice more, the Pladson sheep returned. But luckily, Jocey was at home, ready for them. She chased them off before they could do any damage. Now that they'd had a taste of her gardens, she was afraid they would become regular pests. It was a trial to keep constant watch. She hated the idea, but she knew that sooner or later she would have to go to the Pladsons and tell them to keep their sheep home.

On top of the sheep troubles and all her hard work, Gram's charade, her pretense of being sick, was getting to be just too much. Jocey had a harder and harder time fighting against the steaming, underground volcano that was her resentment.

On a day that was hot by ten in the morning, Jocey labored in the kitchen with yellow soap and a washboard, doing their wash. With a lot of begging, she had persuaded Gram to do the baking for a change. Only Gram didn't have the strength to stir the flour and yeast as it turned out, and Jocey had to do it. Gram couldn't knead the dough, either, and she had done that, too. Now Gram sat in her chair by the table, watching the bowl of bread dough rise under a shaft of sunlight.

Grandma Letty was in one of her gabby moods, and she prattled on about the people she had known in Kansas City. "Mrs. Molino was the persnickitiest housekeeper I ever did meet," she told Jocey. "She would not do anything that would dirty her house a little extry. Like pie. Told me once she refused to give her man pie. Because making pie was too messy! Ever hear the like?"

Jocey shrugged and went on wringing out the dress she'd sudsed clean.

Mentioning pie must have reminded Gram. "Do we have some a' our mulberry pie left?" she asked.

"Yes we do, Gram. I was saving it for supper."

Her grandmother made a kind of whimper, "I think one of the reasons I just can't get my strength back, is you don't feed me enough—"

"Grandma Letty!" Jocey exploded. "You eat like a—" A sudden knock at the door halted her tongue.

"Comp'ny!" Gram had the look of a child being visited by a circus.

Jocey reacted just the opposite. She looked vainly for her hat, a scarf, or a place to hide. Spotting a dishtowel folded by the dry sink, she grabbed it up and wound it about her head. "I got a toothache," she whispered to her grandmother. "Send whoever it is at the door away if it isn't urgent."

Gram hobbled for the door. A sharp wag of her hand behind her back told that she was not of a mind to let any callers get away and Jocey could shush any objection she might have.

"How do you do, gents!" Jocey heard her grandmother say, as she opened the door wide. "What can I do for you?"

Jocey shrank back against the cupboard. She couldn't see who it was, but the voice from the porch was jovial and booming, "Good morning fair lady! Isn't this a beautiful day? My friend and I are—"

"—road weary, Ma'am," a second voice finished nasally as if on cue. "We saw this cozy homestead from the road. We knew only kind folks could dwell in such a lovely haven."

The first voice took another turn. "We took the liberty of tying our team. May we come in to rest ourselves a spell?" To Jocey's astonishment a man's hand grasped Gram's, lifted it, and kissed it. "With your kind permission, of course?"

Gram ducked her head demurely and stepped back. "'Course you're welcome to come in. We don't know no strangers here." She waved them inside. "Make yourselves comfortable over there at the table. My grandbaby girl, Joee there, will bring you some pie and coffee to have while you're restin'. An' we'll just visit, all righty?"

With held breath, Jocey watched suspiciously as the strangers came inside. The first man, short and stocky in a striped suit and bow tie, didn't look one bit tired as he swung jauntily into the room. His companion was older and taller. He too wore a fine suit, but he looked somehow untidy, and not from travel, it was more just *him*. Why had they come here? This wasn't a road ranch, an inn.

She shriveled inside and her heartbeat quickened when the shorter man took note of her. He hurried over, clucking his tongue, "Toothache? Put some oil of cloves on it, daughter. That will ease the pain." Under heavy brows his blue eyes twinkled and he bowed low. "The name is Andrew Smith. It's a pleasure to meet you, darlin'."

Jocey felt less afraid, but she still didn't like their being here. Why didn't they take their honeyed tongues and go away? She mumbled, "If you are tired and need a meal, neither Bushong nor Allen nor Council Grove is very far from here."

Gram looked at her, horrified. She stomped her foot. "Joee Belle Royal where's your manners? Get them that pie that was left. Stir the fire under the coffee." She turned to beam at the taller visitor who was introducing himself as Wallace Kipper. "Sit, Mr. Kipper, sit."

Couldn't her grandmother see that these men wouldn't be so friendly to perfect strangers if they weren't up to something? Jocey was sure they were after more than wanting to rest. Yet, for the next twenty minutes or more, the men visited companionably with Gram. They sipped their coffee, ate, and listened politely to Gram telling how she and Jocey came to be in the Neosho Valley.

The men nodded and sat back smiling. They answered that this area was prosperous, far more beautiful farm country than they had seen anywhere else, and they had traveled far and wide.

Was that it, did they want to buy the farm?

Then, Andrew Smith finally interrupted a long-winded story of Gram's to say, "Yes, this is paradise, ladies. You seem to have every worldly need in this little cottage." He looked about.

"Except—" Wallace Kipper lifted a hand—"a sewing machine. I don't believe these fine ladies have a sewing machine, Andrew." His nasal whine made it sound as though not having a sewing machine was the worst thing in the world.

Jocey was disgusted. Why didn't they come right out at the beginning and say they were sewing machine salesmen? Why all the pussyfooting around? She and Gram couldn't afford to buy one. She loosened the towel slightly so there would be no mistaking her words, "We do our sewing by hand. We don't need a sewing machine."

Andrew Smith leaped to his feet, then, like he was a performer on a stage. "It's clear, daughter, that you have not had the opportunity to see what the famous Maxwell sewing machine can do. Now, we just happen to have one out in the buggy. May we bring it in, to demonstrate? It'll take but a minute."

Jocey shook her head in protest, but Kipper advised her, "Every woman in the land wants a modern sewing machine. And the Maxwell machine is the invention of the century."

"We don't have the money to buy one." Her voice came muffled but intentionally strong from under the dishtowel. "We don't want to waste your time."

"Wait now, wait," Gram cried. "I want to see it, Joee. I do. Just a look. I'd admire to sew thataway, like the fine ladies in Kansas City do. It won't hurt to look at it, and someday maybe we can buy one. We'll know how to work a sewing machine, after today."

The salesmen's eyes met. Their expressions told Jocey that they believed a sale had the same as been made. They hurried out the door together, smiling.

How could she get rid of them? Jocey's shoulders drooped, and she slumped into a chair, her swaddled jaw in her hand. It would upset Gram, but they really ought to send these smooth-talkers on their way. All at once, Jocey knew a way. She removed the towel from her head and face and sat with it in her lap, waiting for the salesmen to come back inside.

Kipper, red-faced and puffing, carried the sewing machine into the kitchen. "Put it right there by the table!" Andrew Smith said, rubbing his hands together.

They took no note of Jocey who waited in the chair with her mouth exposed, wishing the fools would hurry and look her way.

"Think of it ladies. Because of marvelous technology, thanks to our nation's finest inventive minds, you can now be free from the drudgery of the needle forever." Andrew Smith's fingertips as he spoke went over the settled, shiny black machine like he was sorting jewels.

"We can't afford the sewing machine," Jocey said loudly from her corner.

Full steam into their spiel, the men ignored her. "—save yourselves precious time for leisure, rest, and refinement," Kipper droned as he trotted about, helping to get the machine ready. "You will see an immediate increase in free time to spend with your beloveds. New avenues to employment will be suddenly opened to you; you can take in sewing, design fashions."

Through clenched teeth Jocey warned, "This is wasting time—"

Nobody seemed to hear her, and they didn't look her way.

"The threaded bobbin goes right here," Andrew Smith said, "and the spool up here starts the thread along the arm of your machine, you see." He looked up. "This we call the—" His speech died in his throat as he stared at Jocey. In a moment he lowered his glance.

When Smith stopped talking, Wallace Kipper looked around curiously and saw Jocey. He flinched, but that didn't surprise her. She had seen this same reaction, this look of repulsion, a hundred times before in her thirteen years of life.

Mr. Smith was the first to attempt to regain his composure. "Pardon us for—staring. We—we didn't know . . ." He turned his attention to the machine again. "This we call the 'spring of the wire' and it is for—" As though unable to help himself, he looked again at Jocey, thoughtfully. His glance returned again to the machine, but he seemed to have lost his place and his hands fumbled. "Kipper, where were we?" He looked at the older man and ran his tongue over his lips.

Wallace Kipper was having his own troubles. "M-money is n-not a problem. A small down payment, f-five dollars a month, and before you know it"—his top lip began to twitch—"this beautiful, timesaving sewing machine will be yours." He mopped his forehead on his sleeve.

"I fancy it," Gram gloated, unaware of anything in the room save the sewing machine and the marvels she was hearing. "I can count the pretty new dresses I have had the last few years on—" She held up one thumb. "Joee." She finally looked her way but hesitated only slightly. "Come fall you might want to go to that big school in Council Grove. You'd need new clothes. Think how fast this machine could whip up a batch a' pretty frocks?"

Jocey had to give the salesmen credit; their aplomb lost, they nevertheless hung on, and attempted to show Gram how to operate the sewing machine. They had Gram put a dress of Jocey's under the cloth presser, an old one she was in the midst of letting out at the hem.

"Now, the new hem goes right here," Gram spoke to herself. As directed, she began to peddle her feet, treadling triumphantly. But suddenly, the top wheel made a half turn forward, then came back.

"Whoa," Andrew Smith cried nervously, "take it easy, Ma'am."

"It looked so durned easy when you did it," Gram wailed. She pulled on the dress, and there was a faint snap as the needle broke. "Now what in thunder?" she stormed, giving the dress a yank. "Tarnal machine won't work atall."

"Please," Mr. Smith implored, "I can fix everything." He half-lifted Gram away from his machine. He then handed the dress toward Jocey without actually looking at her. "If—if you would pick out the runaway stitches . . ."

Wallace Kipper, agitation plain in his face, replaced the broken needle. Once more, Andrew Smith explained the machine to Gram.

Jocey, near to laughing, didn't listen. Gram tried the machine again. This time she caught the soft pad of her forefinger under the new needle.

"Take the blamed thing away," Gram commanded around the finger she'd stuck in her mouth. "We ain't got no use for it."

"We can leave the machine with you for a week or two, allow you to practice and get used to it," Mr. Smith offered.

Gram was shaking her head, but she was turned away, and Jocey couldn't see her face. She didn't know how Gram really felt. The sewing machine would be wonderful to have. She reconsidered, "Gram, if you'd really like to buy the sewing machine, there is your burying money we could spend."

Gram whirled to face her, and she looked like she might be having a relapse before Jocey's eyes. "No. Not my buryin' money. I—I ain't that pert."

Maybe Gram was just tired. She did look bad. For sure she was running short on patience as she pointed to the sewing machine and told the men, "We don't want it. We ain't got the money to buy it, and it's dangerous, anyhow. Get it on out of here."

"We could take old jewelry or a gun in trade," Kipper persisted. "If you have something like that, I can take a look?"

"We have only one reason for showing anybody our gun," Jocey said.

"Ah. Ah, I see," Kipper stammered. He signaled with a motion of his head to Andrew Smith. "We have taken enough of these ladies' time." He picked up the machine and lugged it toward the door, muttering under his breath something that sounded to Jocey like, "simpleminded country bumpkins."

Her ire rose, even as Smith said, "It's been delightful talking to you, even if we couldn't do business." He spoke without looking at her or Gram and might have been talking to his sewing machine.

"Goodbye," Jocey said, her tone as civil as she could manage.

At the door, Smith turned to look back at her, his glance flitting from her mouth to her eyes, then to her mouth again. "I—I am sorry about th-that, sure too bad." He acted ready to say more, but he didn't.

"It's none of your worry." Jocey went to hold the door open.

Out in the yard, Kipper grunted his way to the buggy where he stowed the machine behind the seat and climbed in. When he saw Andrew Smith still standing with Jocey on the porch, he shook his head. His expression was dour as he took up the reins and turned his team and buggy about. "Smith, are you coming?"

"About your h-handicap . . ." Andrew Smith began.

Jocey was shocked, then fighting mad. "I know all about my mouth! It has been with me this way all of my life, after all. And if you think you are the first person to notice it—"

"I—I didn't mean . . ." he protested lamely.

"It doesn't matter one whit what you meant. *Goodbye,* Mr. Smith. Take your sewing machine on down the road. Bother somebody else. The Pladsons live yonder." She waved her arm wildly. "They have a lot of children. They might use one of your machines." She rushed inside and slammed the door, then leaned against it, swallowing back the ache in her throat. The nerve of him, wanting to come right out in the open and talk about her mouth! Out of morbid curiosity, for sure.

CHAPTER 9

"You wasn't very nice, Joee," Grandma Letty accused half-heartedly when the sewing machine salesmen had departed. She examined the empty, berry-stained pie plate with a regretful frown.

"Oh, I know I wasn't, Gram, but I couldn't help it." Jocey went back to take up the washing where she'd left off. So much to do, so much time wasted with Kipper and Smith. "Someday we will have more money, Gram," she prophesied, "and we'll buy us a sewing machine. But it won't be from glib-tongued, weak-kneed fools the likes of them we met today."

"Smith didn't seem so bad. It looked to me like he was real sorry for you."

Jocey didn't answer. Maybe he was sorry for her, but she hated pity. Staring at her the way he did was—nasty. But then, she realized, it was she who had showed herself barefaced, just asking for trouble.

Within a few days, Jocey could remember the sewing machine salesmen's visit without feeling angry and hurt. They seemed a funny, ridiculous pair to her now, and she almost wished them luck, selling their machines.

Then one day as she was trying to chase down one of Opal's half-grown chicks, escaped from the henhouse, she heard the snort of horses and the creaking of a buggy from the direction of their lane. She looked, first thinking to vanish into the barn. But the lone person in the buggy had seen her and was waving. *Papa?* For a second her heart seemed to stop, then she recognized the buggy, and Andrew Smith. Her spirits dipped. Why was he coming back here by himself?

"Halloo," he called out as he came closer, "ain't this a day for livin' though?"

Jocey stood with her hat pulled low and her hands on her hips. The salesman drew his team to a halt a few feet away. He leaped from the buggy and strode toward her, smiling.

"I told you we couldn't buy your sewing machine." Then she asked incredulously, when he leaned down to stare into her face without shame, "You come back for a good look? A bear did it, you know, I was eating a grizzly bear alive, and he clawed me going down."

"Sweet young lady, don't talk like that." His tone, gentle and soft, unsettled Jocey. "I did come back to talk to you about your—affliction. But never to make fun of you."

If tormenting wasn't it, what could there be left to talk about? It angered Jocey that his kind way should make her feel like this—helpless, exposed. She tried to speak, to order him off her land, but she couldn't say a word. Instead, she looked down at her bare feet, and her chin trembled.

"There is something I have to tell you, Miss. Something I can't get out of my mind. I was in the neighborhood anyway. Collecting payments for machines."

She looked up. "If this is about your sewing machines—"

He shook his head, and now she saw the look of excitement in his eyes. "No. Like I said, this is about you—about your mouth. Daughter, I know of a person who had an *operation*. For a problem like yours." He plunged on, "This person had a harelip, and it was fixed! I thought you ought to know about it. Only the once did I hear about this operation being done. But you're such a pretty girl otherwise, and . . ."

The barnyard was beginning to spin dizzily around her. "What did you say?" Jocey whispered. "What did you say about my mouth?" It was hard to breathe; her middle felt as though the butt end of a log had struck it. *An operation?*

"I said I believe your mouth can be fixed."

His face faded in a blur of sudden tears. She pressed a closed fist against her mouth to keep from crying out, and she shook her head. It couldn't be true. Such a miracle could never be. She waited for Andrew Smith to say more, because her own throat was too tight for words.

"I heard, *saw* this child who had had a mouth like yours, a harelip," he repeated. "She'd had an operation. This was while I was on one of my selling trips. I can't recall just where I was at the time, or the name of the people. I might have been in Topeka, or maybe it was Saint Louis. I just don't know." He scratched his head. "The fact that there is such an operation, that's what's important. Something was in the back of my mind from the minute I saw you had a—a harelip. But it didn't come clear to me until after I'd left that it was the possibility of an operation that was bothering me."

"Please don't lie to me about this if it isn't true, please," Jocey begged. "You're not just trying to soften me up so we'll buy a machine?" Even as she spoke, Jocey regretted the words. She knew, deep down, that it was true, Smith wasn't lying. *Her mouth could be fixed!* Suddenly awash with hope and dreams, the desire to look normal like others, made her weak. She reached for the salesman's arm. "Help me. What can I do? Where can I go to get this—the operation?"

He gripped her hand and smiled. "As soon as Kipper and I sell the sewing machines we have on hand, we have to go back to the city for more. There are hospitals there, and all kinds of doctors. I'll ask around and find out what I can. I'll be back to tell you what I learn. All right?"

Since she didn't know any other way to find out by herself, Jocey nodded. "I was awful rude to you and your partner. We didn't buy from you. You didn't have to come back. You don't owe me anything like this."

"As one human being to another, I owe you." Andrew Smith grinned. "If you won't accept that, then maybe you'll be happy to know that your neighbors, the Pladsons, bought a machine from us, after you sent us there so speedily. I've got to go over there now to ask for a payment."

Jocey could hardly think straight, let alone know what to say, and he left soon after. But in her heart a small flame of hope she'd never known before flickered and grew bright. To be normal—to be normal. Nice lips, a straight mouth. Did she dare to dream it?

From that moment, Jocey's every thought and action was colored by the new hope. Until she could be sure about the operation, though, she would keep it a secret, she decided. On the other hand, holding the excitement within was almost as tiring as hard physical work.

Surely such an operation would take an enormous amount of money. She began to worry. Would her gardens bring in enough? To try to make sure, she nurtured each vegetable plant with even greater care. Sometimes she talked to them, begging a corn stalk or tomato plant to produce as none ever had before. She knew she was being foolish, but desperation drove her to try anything that might help.

Worrying that Mr. Smith might be wrong made her sleep fitful. She had never heard of such an operation, and she was positive Gram hadn't either. If you were born with a harelip, you kept it all your life, and that was that. Smith had seemed honest enough, though, that last visit. He felt sorry for her, too, but she didn't want that. All she wanted was for him to bring her the *right* message. And she wanted to have money enough to pay for the miracle operation.

Within their boundary and beyond Fox Creek there were several acres of wild hay. Jocey began to cut and stack it with the hope of selling some, since there was far more than she needed for Nappy. But the long, hard days cutting hay, and near sleepless nights, began to tell on her.

There were times, going to bed, when she felt like a sunbaked, half-dead corpse crawling into a coffin not to come out. Yet her mind, dwelling always on the possibility of the operation, was too feverishly alive with wanting to allow her sleep. After one such night spent tossing and turning, she overslept. Even when she woke, she felt weighted to the bed. When she went outside, after breakfast, feeling sore and rubbing her eyes to open them, the sun was high. And the Pladson sheep were trampling her cornfield.

Her brief horror turned to near insane anger. They couldn't! She looked about for something to whip the sheep with, or to throw at them, and saw nothing. She raced for the potato patch where the plants were curled and brown, but where fat potatoes rested under the surface of the soft soil. Whimpering, she began to scratch the potatoes out with her fingers. She clawed them up into her arms and then rushed to hurtle one potato after another at the sheep, as hard as she could throw.

"Leave my corn be!" she screeched. "Get out of here. Go home. Stay home, you worthless critters!" Her breath caught in a sob. She had waited too long to tell the Pladsons to keep their sheep off her land. She needed the corn to sell for the operation, and now— Jocey choked back sobs that ached for release.

Finally she got the sheep hazed out of the corn and headed homeward. Their blatting still echoed in her mind as she hurried to the barnyard where she threw a blanket on Nappy. She would ride to the Pladsons' this day.

Jocey took only a moment at the house to yell

through the open kitchen door to Grandma, "I'll be back by noon. You fix dinner today, Grandma, please!" Then she was off, riding Nappy at a trot, on south to the Pladsons'. She knew their farm from making rounds selling her vegetables and had seen from the road that they had their own huge garden. She'd never stopped in. Now she must!

When she rode into the Pladson yard, Jocey's anger still burned to the point where she almost didn't care if they saw her face. She tied Napoleon to a post near the well and watering trough and strode across the dusty, shaded yard. At the kitchen door, she raised her fist, but before she could pound, the door opened.

The woman facing her was short and squat; her wide, smooth face broke into a quick, questioning smile. "Yes? You want some'ting?" She reached up to tuck wisps of hair back into the thick gold braids wound about her head, and she asked, "Is trouble?" She tried peeking into the shadows caused by Jocey's hat brim over her face.

"You are Mrs. Pladson?" Jocey's knees felt suddenly weak as she recalled Mr. Pladson's warning that she must never come near his family.

The woman nodded and held the door open wider. "*Yah,* I am Thea Pladson, Edvard's wife. You come in, please." She gestured.

Jocey took a few uncertain steps into the room and halted. "I don't like to complain," she began, "but your husband's sheep are ruining my crops. Most of the time I've been able to keep watch and chase them away before they could do much damage. But they keep coming back. This morning they ruined a third, maybe half, of my corn."

Mrs. Pladson grimaced and wrung her hands. "Oh, no. No! I am so sorry. We know our sheep wander from time to time. We not know about any damage they do. We must keep them home, yes. My child, you live where?"

"I'm Jocelyn Belle Royal and I live—" she broke off, startled by Thea Pladson's near fit of joy. The woman grasped her arm and tugged her along into the next room, making soft exclamations Jocey couldn't understand.

In the room, a blonde girl about eleven years old sat at a sewing machine identical to the one Smith and Kipper had brought to their house. "Is my daughter, Anne." Mrs. Pladson introduced her proudly.

The young girl was beautiful, Jocey thought. Something inside herself shriveled from envy. She jerked her glance away to look at the fat blonde baby sitting on a quilt on the floor, playing with a string of empty spools.

"Baby there is Kari," said Mrs. Pladson. "Our sons, Tosten and Nils, will want to meet you, too, but they are in the fields with Edvard." She drew a breath and exclaimed, "Anne, this girl is Jim Royal's child. The girl, Jocelyn. Do you remember? Mr. Royal talked about his Jocey."

They knew her?

Anne stood up quickly, putting her sewing aside. She smiled. "Of course, I remember, Mama." She ducked her small head in a semblance of a curtsy. "Your Papa talked about you all the time. We thought it was you, come to live on the farm. We hoped we'd get to know you, but our Papa . . ." her voice trailed off, and she shrugged.

Jocey's mind spun, all of this was so unexpected, so sudden. "You—you knew my father well?" she asked when she could.

Anne nodded. She leaned forward and whispered, "He brought us books. He taught us how to read English in his books."

Jocey's puzzlement must have shown.

"My Edvard, he don't understand," Mrs. Pladson told her. "He does not like the learning from books for his children."

"Whyever not?" Jocey was astonished.

"Because he think it spoil them for good hard work. I try to tell him different. In Oslo, my old home, is all right to have books. But Edvard and other immigrants who come to this new land long ago when they were small, all they know is the hard work."

Anne told her, "Girls are supposed to work in the house and with the chickens and geese, and in the garden. My brothers' place is in the fields and barn. Papa thinks if we do our work as we should, there is not time for books."

"I—I think that's sad," Jocey whispered. What would her life be, without books?

Mrs. Pladson spread her palms up to the sky. "What can I say? He is head of house and a good man in his heart."

Jocey was thoughtful a moment. "Books, then, must have something to do with why your husband is mad at Papa. Why he doesn't want me to come here."

Mrs. Pladson looked distressed. "If he say not to come here, that is reason. Jim Royal and my Edvard have a bad fight one time. Almost to raising their fists to one another. Terrible argument, they have. About the books they not agree at all. Edvard order your Papa not to come here. Jim thought Edvard was wrong. He still give us books when he could."

Inside, Jocey felt a kind of ease and joy. "I knew Papa couldn't have done anything very wrong. I can see how he would feel. He was a teacher once, you know. I love books, too."

"In Oslo," Mrs. Pladson said with a nod, "girls from good homes are taught how to read. I can read. I read many of your father's books. But it has been a long time . . ."

Jocey started to ask if they might know where her father had gone, but Anne Pladson spoke, "You are just the way your Papa said you were. Uh-pretty," she added uncomfortably after a moment's hesitation. And then, "He was so sad for you." Anne's fingers crept up to her own pretty mouth.

Papa had told them about *that?* And they understood? Neither Anne nor Mrs. Pladson acted uncomfortable about her handicap. Jocey felt a kind of lightening, a new softness inside. Were these—could these be—friends?

"Your Papa missed you very much. He wanted to bring you and your mother to the farm, he was so excited. He worked very hard getting it ready. And then your poor mother—" Mrs. Pladson looked stricken, and she quickly changed the subject, "When your Papa come here, he say to my young ones, 'You practice enough and someday you be as fine a reader as my Jocey.' He love you so much."

Jocey allowed the words, and all they meant, to sink in. Of course, all this was before Mama's death. He had to go—he had to try to get away, from the hurt. Tears stung the corners of her eyes. She blinked them away and asked, "Do you know where my Papa went? I haven't heard from him for two years, going on three, now. Do you have any idea where he might be?"

Mrs. Pladson looked surprised. A shadow seemed to cross her face.

CHAPTER 10

"Your father went to Mexico. Did you know that?" Mrs. Pladson's voice was gentle.

Feeling stunned and confused, Jocey allowed herself to be drawn toward a pair of chairs where they sat down. She examined her hands in her lap a moment and slowly shook her head. "After Mama died, Papa went out west for a while. He came to Kansas City a few times after that, to visit Gram and me. Then, about two years ago, Papa just—kind of vanished. That's all I know." She looked up then and quickly lowered her face again. "He—he went to Mexico?"

"Yah, he went there to work in the oil fields with a man he meet here in the valley. We hear later that the people in Mexico have some trouble. The dictator, Dìaz, they say is his name, rule with an iron hand, but he does not care enough about the common people. The Indians work very hard and have nothing. The well-to-do get richer and richer and not work so hard, if at all. There are small outbreaks of fighting and some say there will be a war—" Mrs. Pladson's voice climbed with alarm and excitement.

Jocey broke in, "But—? *Papa,* what has this to do with him?" A premonition brought chills to her spine. She recalled the nightmare she'd had on the journey from Kansas City. Papa reaching for her, calling her name. He wanted to come home but was being held back, in the dream. Only a dream, but now— "What happened to Papa? Is he dead?"

A frown creased Thea Pladson's brow, and she clucked her tongue. "No. At least we don't know that for sure." She reached for Jocey's hand and patted it. "Your Papa was wounded in a gunfight. He get an infection and was very sick for a long, long time. I don't like to tell you this, but is true."

Jocey's senses, every fiber of her body, began to scream. "But if he isn't dead, where is he? Who told you all this?"

"Ned Block, your Papa's friend, came back to this valley about six months ago, and he tell us. For some months, like a year maybe, Ned was separated from your Papa in Mexico, after your Papa got shot. He could not find your father when he went back to look for him, later. Ned came back to America then. He told us he didn't know if Jim—"

Jocey stood up. "Where is this Ned Block? I want to talk to him. I have to know about Papa. Everything. If he's alive, he may need us."

Thea Pladson frowned. "Ned Block didn't stay around very long before he leave Kansas again." She shook her head. "Maybe he went back to Mexico. I do not know."

"Nobody told me Papa was in Mexico!" Jocey cried, unable to hide her inner turmoil. "If he's been hurt, that's why he hasn't written. There was a lawyer trying to find out where Papa went, didn't he ask you, a neighbor?"

Mrs. Pladson spread her hands. "Nobody ask me about your father, or I would have told them. If they ask my Edvard, he might not say; he is stubborn like a mule. But the little we know about Jim not much good, I think. Mexico is a big place, *big*." She shrugged her plump shoulders. "I am sorry, Jocelyn."

Papa shot in Mexico—the silly feud over books, her mind dragged from one bewildering disclosure back to the other. There must be something she could do for Papa; people she could write to and find out about him. But where to begin? As Mrs. Pladson said, Mexico was a big place, and she knew so little about where in Mexico he might be. Papa could even be dead. *No!* She refused to even think it. Papa was alive. Someday he would come home and find his farm and her and Gram waiting. She knew it!

"I—I better go now," Jocey told the Pladsons. "I wish I hadn't needed to bother you about the sheep, but I am very glad I came."

Anne looked pleadingly at her mother and bounced up and down on her toes, *"Mor,* can we try again? Let's talk Papa into allowing Jocey to bring us books!" She turned to Jocey, "My brother Nils, who is seventeen, loves to read. But then, so does Tosten. He is fifteen. Besides going fishing once in a while and to town to trade, it's work, work, work all the time, and—" She quieted when her mother gave her a warning look.

"These modern children, they different," Mrs. Pladson said with an embarrassed, yet proud, smile. "Some changes good. Edvard someday feel different about books, I think. I will keep trying, to help him see."

"I hope he does change his mind," Jocey told them. "If he does, please remember that I have lots of Papa's books at the farm, and some of my own that I'll gladly loan." It might be all right, yes, it would be wonderful to have the Pladsons visit her and Gram. The way they treated her, it was different, and nice. She'd like to know them even better. They could get to know her and Gram, too. She watched the baby, sucking on the spools, looking like a fat sweet cherub, and her arms ached to hold her.

Mrs. Pladson said, "You keep looking at the baby. You want to hold Kari?" She bustled toward the infant and reached down to pick her up.

"Oh, no," Jocey protested hastily, "I can't." They looked at her, puzzled. Did she need to explain? "It's my face, I would scare her."

"Nah, not Kari," Mrs. Pladson said staunchly. "She love to be held. Here, you take the child and not to worry." She thrust the baby into Jocey's arms.

A wonderful feeling swept through Jocey as she held the soft, sweet-smelling infant against her. Hesitantly, she pressed her cheek atop the baby's silky head. "I love her."

Anne giggled and clasped her hands.

Thea Pladson laughed heartily, "See? Is all right!"

Later, as Jocey was going out the door, Mrs. Pladson tapped her lips. "We know about this. Your Papa tell us. It does not matter, you don't worry about it here. You come see us again and next time we have some fresh *lefse,* or *fattigan bakels* for you."

"Norwegian food," Anne interpreted, jouncing on her hip the baby Jocey had reluctantly handed over. "*Lefse* is soft bread, buttered and folded like half a pie and folded again into a triangle so you eat it like a sandwich. *Fattigan bakels*—like doughnuts."

"Thank you ever so much. I—I will come again if I can. Please, come see us, too." She'd just made,

Jocey realized, the first truly honest move to be sociable she had ever made in her life. It wasn't hard. Why had she waited so long? Because so few people had treated her as kindly as the Pladsons did, perhaps. In that moment, it was like a pleasant, exciting door opening for her. On the porch, Jocey turned to look back.

Mrs. Pladson and Anne were both crowded into the doorway, waving. "You not to worry about the sheep," the mother called. "I tell Nils and Tosten straight away they must see to the fences, keep sheep home."

"Thank you," Jocey called back. In spite of her worry over Papa, she felt good. A small giggle bubbled up from inside her as she mounted Nappy. To think, she'd come here to the Neosho Valley farm to hide, and she'd found friends!

In the far cornfield off to her left, two tall blond boys halted shucking corn to watch Jocey ride by. Nils. Tosten. It was the younger of the two, Tosten, she thought, who'd come by the creek that day carrying the fish pole. His face was still an indelible picture in her mind.

Jocey couldn't see the boys' father, Edvard Pladson, about. She was just as glad. There was still him to deal with, but the Pladson womenfolk were just plain nice.

Next morning, Jocey sang softly as she finished her chores about the barn, a tune she'd heard

Gram sing often in Kansas City, working over her washtubs:

> *"Oh, Charlie he's a fine young man*
> *Oh, Charlie he's a dandy;*
> *Charlie likes to kiss the gals,*
> *And he can do it handy!*
>
> *Oh, I don't want none o' yore weevily wheat*
> *'An I don't want none o' yore barley*
> *But I want some flour in half an hour*
> *To bake a cake for Charlie."*

"Good morning," a young male voice interrupted her continued humming.

Jocey's hand, tossing feed to Opal and her brood, froze in the air. Slowly, she turned, clasping the feedpan against her apron. A blond boy in clean but worn overalls and faded shirt stood there. At the opposite end of the rope he held in his hand stood a large yellow cow placidly chewing her cud. The boy's other hand was held behind his back.

Except for the lopsided grin, he very much favored Mrs. Pladson and Anne.

"What do you want?" Jocey asked, her old stiffness returning. He was such a fine-looking boy. While she, by comparison . . . Her heart ached.

"I'm Tosten Pladson. And this is Gertrude. Trudy is a fine milker."

"I'm Jocelyn Royal." She kept her face lowered. Her feet shifted of their own accord, and she fought an urge to flee. Curiosity held her. It didn't seem reasonable that he would bring his cow here for her to meet. But what else? "Your cow is beautiful," she told him, swallowing hard.

"I brought her for you. *Mor* said."

This must be a joke. Jocey peeked up at him from the corner of her eye, to see if this was some new form of teasing.

"*Mor*—my mother, sent Trudy to you. For loan as long as you want, in payment for the damage our flock of sheep did to your crops." He grinned, "And these are from me because I was supposed to watch the sheep." From behind his back he held out a nosegay of blue larkspur and pink sweet william.

Jocey's eyes went wide in surprise, her face, lifted, turned warm. "I—I can't take Trudy—"

He motioned with his head to where Napoleon grazed in the pasture beyond the barn. "Shall I put Trudy in the field with your horse, or do you want me to put her in the barn?" Seeing Jocey still shaking her head, Tosten spoke mockingly solemn, "*Mor* insists. She'll hit me if I bring Trudy back home again."

Jocey laughed. She took a few steps forward, took the flowers, and stroked the cow's warm yellow side. Her tortured feelings inside evaporated, and she whispered, "I'm not sure the sheep did so much damage that your mother's cow is fair payment. But they did do plenty." If she had this cow, she could sell milk, butter, and cheese. The money would help so much for her mouth—the operation if it came to pass. "Would you put her in with Nappy, my horse? Th-thank you for the bouquet."

To Tosten's lean straight back, as he coaxed Trudy along in the direction of the pasture, she said, "I'll take care of Trudy like she's my own cow. And—and thank your mother and father for me. I'm ever so grateful. When they want to have her back, they are just to say so." The friendliness in his grin as he looked back over his shoulder encouraged Jocey to tag along, slowly.

Like his mother and sister, Tosten Pladson didn't seem upset by her handicap. The revelation felt like chains coming unbroken from around her, freeing her to be her own true self. Her heart climbed into her throat as she saw the boy coming back to the fence where she waited, as if he wanted to talk to her. Partly she had Papa to thank; whatever he had told the Pladson family about her had helped ease the way. She was grateful to them, too, because their simple kindness and openness about her mouth made it easier for her. "Thank you for bringing Trudy over."

Tosten shrugged. "I didn't mind. It got me away from shucking corn for a while." He climbed the fence and sat straddling it, chewing a blade of grass.

"We don't get out much to visit our neighbors," he confessed. "Don't have much to do with anybody." His happy expression of earlier was gone, as he told her, "I wish I could start to school on time this fall, but *Far,* my father, only lets us go to school when he doesn't need us at home. If *Mor* didn't teach us at home, ciphering and things like that, we'd be such dunderheads."

Jocey felt akin to him in his problem, for she'd gone to school so little, too, when she wanted otherwise. "I understand that my Papa taught you to read English, and he lent you books?"

Tosten shook his head, "It's been a long time, now. But I remember—" He stroked his arm and looked at the ground, thinking, "There was a book of your father's called, I think—*The Dog Of Flanders* or *Flanders Dog.* It was too hard for me to read, before, but I would like to try again."

"*A Dog Of Flanders;* it's in the house. If you want it, come on in."

He beamed at Jocey, dropped off the fence, and strode beside her as she headed for the house. "I'll have to hide it from *Far,*" he said, "and I might have to keep it awhile. Nils and Anne and *Mor* will want to read it, too."

"Sure." If there was to be a bond between them, then she was glad it was books. Jocey led him up the back steps to the porch. In the kitchen, it startled her to see Gram busily cleaning up their breakfast dishes. Gram didn't lift a finger to help anymore, and now . . . Momentarily shocked, Jocey wondered, *what possesses Gram today?* She pushed the question to the back of her mind with the hope that whatever had gotten into Gram, it would last.

"Grandma Letty, this is Tosten Pladson." From the pail of water on the wash bench, Jocey dipped a jar of water for her flowers. "He wants to borrow a book of Papa's."

Grandma seemed nonplussed that she'd been caught in a rare act of helping. Nevertheless, she shook the dishpan suds from her fingers and grabbed Tosten's young brown paw into her own. "My granddaughter Joee tells me your Mama was very nice to her yesterday. Joee says your family knew my Kathleen's husband, Jim Royal? An' he's gotten into some trouble down in Mexico? An' he's missing—" She shook her head. "Son, I'd like to set a spell and visit with your Mama, would you tell her? You folks are more than welcome to come see us. 'Specially Sunday afternoons. That's when it's mighty quiet around here, Joee sittin' with her head in a book. Me with nothing to do but twiddle my thumbs in idleness."

Jocey nearly choked, hearing Gram's last words. She saw Tosten's sincere grin.

"*Mor* wants you to come calling at our house, too. *Far*"—he appeared embarrassed—"might not be there when you come, though. He keeps very busy in the fields and—all."

Jocey couldn't hold back her good news any longer. "Mrs. Pladson lent us a cow, Gram, in exchange for the damage the sheep did!"

Grandma clapped her cheeks in delight. "We can have cream and butter? Oh, my! I'll teach you how to milk, Joee, this very day." She hesitated then, as though looking inward—possibly at some decision she'd come to. "No." She changed her mind. "I will do the milking my own self from now on. You got aplenty to do, Joee." She examined her wrinkled hands, tops and palms. "It's been a mighty long while since I've had my hands on a cow." She flexed her fingers. "But these old hands'll remember what to do."

Such forward talk from her own grandmother, in front of Tosten, made Jocey blush. "I'll get the book for you," she said quickly and hurried into the front room.

When she came back, Gram and Tosten were excitedly exchanging boasts about cows.

"—milk full to the brim of a bucket and three inches of cream on top," Tosten was saying, his young face just inches from her grandmother's.

"Bucket and a half and *five* inches of cream, our Flossie used to give," Gram countered, smacking a fist into her other palm.

Tosten shrugged. His eyes twinkled as he turned to Jocey and grinned. "She wins."

Jocey held her mouth firm to lessen the effect of

her handicap, but her eyes laughed back at Tosten.

When he left, *A Dog Of Flanders* stuffed inside his shirt, Gram went back to scouring the oatmeal pot in her pan of suds. She echoed Jocey's very thoughts, "If the rest of the family is like that boy, we got good neighbors, Joee."

She nodded. Now—if the father wouldn't be such a grump . . .

CHAPTER 11

It took a while, but Grandma Letty milked the big yellow cow, Trudy, that night. Afterward, she showed Jocey how to set the milk in flat pans on a table at the shadier end of their enclosed back porch. "Cream will rise to the top," Gram informed her, "and then we skim it off for making butter. If I can recollect how it's done, I will make us some cheese, too."

This further evidence of a switchabout in Gram made Jocey itch to know what had brought it on. It might be one of those small miracles, though, she thought, that a person should just be thankful for and not question.

With no prodding, Gram made her confession that

same night. They sat in the yard trying to cool off, after chores and supper. "I've done got tired a' sittin' on my backside doing nothing, Joee," she said, breaking their companionable silence. "I know you wouldn't a' known it to look at me, but I've been feeling pert for quite a spell now. I ought to've helped you more than I done."

"Well, Gram—" Jocey cleared her throat.

Grandma Letty waved her silent and explained, "You see, Joee, I been a hard worker, a *hard worker,* all of my life. Never had a chance to loaf, till I got sick and you got to takin' care of me. That was the nicest thing ever happened to me. Being waited on by you, Grandbaby." She chuckled softly. "I think I got to relishing it too much and didn't want it to stop. It was hard to face that I was well, but I can't fool myself no longer."

"But you are better, Gram, and that's what counts."

"I'm going to help, Joee, from now on. It's me and you together. Milkin' that Trudy cow tonight kind of carried me back to the times . . ." Her voice trailed off dreamily.

"Tell me about it, Gram," Jocey begged. "I'd love to hear about when you were a girl and lived on a farm."

"It ain't a fancy story." Gram sat in silence a moment, before she went on. "My mam and pap migrated from Kentucky to Missouri with us children when I was a tad. We all worked like mules on that hardscrabble farm. Then, when I was a young gal, not much older than you, I got me a streak of uppity-ness. Thought I'd never marry me a good man if I stayed where I was."

"That's when you went to Kansas City?"

There was guilt and sadness in Gram's reply. "Right in the middle of harvest when my poor old parents needed me the most, I took off. For what? I hated what I found in the city. Never did get to live the fancy life I favored. In time, I was too ashamed of what I'd done to go home again. I married Horace, your grandpappy. He was a kind man, but weak."

"Didn't you ever go back home, even once?" Jocey asked.

"When my man died, I thought about going back." She shook her head. "But I'd heard that my mam and pap were gone to their graves. My brothers and sisters had scattered like leaves in a wind. The bank had took the farm back. No, Joee, I never did see my family again. And that ain't right. People ought not to cut theirselves off from loved ones, never. It's a thing that's sorried me all my life."

"You do have some family, Gram, *me*. And the more I think about it, the more I just know Papa will come home again. You'll have him, too."

"You're a good girl, Joee." Gram reached over and rubbed Jocey's shoulder. "I been thinking a lot lately; it's wrong what I been doing to you, being a burden. Not helping when I was able. The jinx I put on you was nigh enough. Enough."

Just one other time, before they left Kansas City, had Gram mentioned this jinx, or hex. "Gram, I wish you'd tell me about that, the—the jinx."

The time must have come when Grandma wanted to get a lot off her chest, Jocey thought, for Gram hesitated only a second before she answered, "It was the uppityness. Leavin' my people thataway was the beginning. From then on my luck was sour. Married the sorriest sort of fella a girl could hitch herself to. Then my only child was born with weak lungs and didn't get to live to be hardly a woman. Poor Kathleen. Her baby, you, come born with a harelip an' that's my fault, too." She sighed heavily, "Just more punishment for what I done."

Jocey felt sorry for Gram and her foolish beliefs. "Grandma, my mouth isn't like this because of anything you did. These things just happen. Life is like that." She was dying to tell Grandma Letty that there was a chance that her mouth could be fixed with an operation. Knowing about it would help Gram feel better. But if Smith came back and said he was mistaken—No. She didn't want anybody but herself to be disappointed. She would wait alone for word from Andrew Smith. Until she knew for sure.

"Gram, you are happy here, aren't you?"

"That I am, Joee, that I am."

Potato harvest began, and still Andrew Smith hadn't come back. With Nappy hitched to the plow, Jocey dug potatoes. Together, she and Gram would pick them up, sort them and put them in bags. Bent over in the row one day, carrying her sack, Gram said, "It ain't a great harvest, but it'll do for somebody new to farmin'."

Jocey had been working vigorously, and she straightened up, panting. She stretched to ease the pain in her back and viewed the gardens. Some rows were a bit crooked, there were bare spots where vegetables hadn't come up, there was a lot of up-and-down-ness to the sizes of the plants. A long way from failure, though. She still believed that gardening was in her blood, that she had a special knack for it. "Harvest'll be better next year, Gram, don't you worry." She had more to go on now than the big almanac book and Gram's advice. She had experience. Her own and others'.

Thea Pladson had come to call on Gram. Both women had enjoyed the visit and others that followed. And Tosten himself told Jocey how to dig a root cellar for storing potatoes, squash, cabbages, and apples for winter.

Edvard Pladson must not agree yet that they should be neighborly, however, Jocey decided, because Tosten and his mother and sisters didn't come often. And when they did, they didn't stay long.

One day in the hayfield, Jocey came around the stack she was building to see Tosten, accompanied by a man she didn't recognize, loping across the stubbled field toward her. She stuck her pitchfork into the ground, leaned wearily against it, and wiped her brow on her sleeve. She yanked her hatbrim low, for the stranger and because the sun was broiling.

In a minute she could see just how agitated Tosten was, as though he was caught in one of the whirlwinds that now and then swept across the field. What in the world? She took a look, then, at the stocky, sunbrowned stranger with him. The man was grinning widely, but the grin began to fade when he came close enough to glimpse her face under the hat's shadows.

"Jocey." Tosten halted and gasped for breath. "This is Ned Block."

She stiffened and stood up straighter.

"He—he," Tosten panted, "he's got good news about your *Far*. Your father. He's alive. Coming home. Wait till you hear—!"

Jocey stared back at Tosten, not uttering a word; knowing she was not reacting the way she was expected to, nor the way she would have thought, herself, that she would, to such good news. It had come so sudden, was so hard to believe . . .

Tosten had a look of exasperation. "Didn't you hear, Jocey? Your father is alive. We think he's coming home."

She wanted to feel something, she wanted to know in her heart that Tosten's words were true, that Papa was all right. After so long, though—Jocey opened her mouth to say something, anything, but still no words would come. The man still stared at her mouth. Jocey saw Tosten give the man a covert nudge.

It seemed to set him in motion. "Don't get the little gal's hopes up," Ned Block said suddenly. His smile flashed off and on again weakly. "This is how it is, Miss," he told Jocey. "I ain't been back to Mexico for a long time. I been living up toward the Nebraska line. But I still got me a beautiful brown-eyed sweetheart down there in Mexico. She don't understand or write very good English, but from the gist of her last letter, I gather your Pa is alive, and ol' Jim is headed for the States. I had written to my gal and some others, hoping for word about him. I come down to these parts to borrow money from some folks of mine—"

"And I saw him," Tosten cut in, "and told him who you were, that you live here now and needed to know about your *Far*."

Ned Block began to laugh, "Reckon you take after your Pa, Miss. Just don't know where you'll find old Jim Royal next." He slapped his thigh. When Jocey didn't laugh and didn't speak, he looked nervous. "Well," he said with a sigh, "we better be gettin' on back, boy."

"Jocey, are you all right?" Tosten asked suddenly. "Aren't you glad about your father?"

She nodded. "Yes, I am." Her voice was husky. "Of course I am glad that Papa's all right." She tried to excuse her numbness, her lack of feeling. "It's the sun. My mind is kind of blank. I've been out here pitching hay since sunup, and I guess I'm too tired to think straight. But if Papa truly is coming back, I'm really ha—" A thickness climbed into her throat, preventing further words.

"It's all right, then." Tosten looked relieved. "You've been working too hard, that's your trouble. Jocey, when you see your *Far* coming down that road over yonder, real as life, you'll believe it then."

"Yes," she said, nodding. "Yes." It was true. When she saw Papa face to face, she would know for a fact he was all right.

After that, Tosten tried to help her with her work whenever he could get away for an hour or two. On one such rare afternoon, they were digging down in the cellar hole, a few yards to the left of the back porch, when the boy began to sing. He made his voice squeak and squawk on purpose, and the silly words were his own. Jocey laughed. She couldn't help but know that Tosten was enjoying himself.

She asked him, before she could stop herself, "Tosten, how come you don't mind being near me? I'm ugly. Other kids have thought I must be feeble-minded because of the way I look. Nobody in Kansas City wanted to be friends with me. But you—"

Tosten quit singing. "Maybe others didn't take time to know you. At first, it did bother me to look at your—face, your mouth. But only a little. I don't hardly see it anymore."

Jocey tensed, her throat dry, "What do you see, Tos-Tosten?" Just saying his name aloud seemed such a tremendous step.

"A girl," he answered quietly. "A girl I knew pretty well even before she came here, because her Pa talked of nothing but her. I see a girl who is handy on the farm, like somebody who has farmed all her life. I see you don't mind the hard work. I see a girl who likes to read books, the same as me. I see—" His voice went shy. "I see you got pretty hair, and the prettiest eyes I ever did see. I suppose, Jocey, I just see *you*."

She knew it then. Even without the operation, Tosten *liked* her. Jocey wanted to tell him that she saw a wonderful, kind boy, but her throat was too full to speak. She'd never know a happier moment than this, she decided. In the dimness of the cellar hole, she reached out and ever so lightly brushed Tosten's arm. His fingers caught hers in a quick squeeze.

The fact that a boy, Tosten Pladson, knew about her mouth—could see it for himself—and still wanted to be friends with her remained a marvel to Jocey for weeks. Her mind was free to consider this new state, though she was busier than ever in the gardens, watering, picking vegetables, and sorting them to sell.

With a feeling of surprise mixed with sadness, she began to think that some of her troubles up to now had been her own doing. It couldn't be denied that others had shunned and rebuffed her, countless times really, due to her deformed mouth. And she knew instinctively it would occur again, many times. Maybe the people who stared or teased or whatever couldn't help the way they behaved, and she was partly to blame. Because, what had she done to change the situation? Change people's minds about her? Hardly anything.

For too long, she saw now, she had let herself be a victim. She had held people off, hid her face, run away—all of that and more. Was it from—fear? Was she afraid that nobody wanted to be the friend of the neighborhood "ugly crip"? She thought so. Because you couldn't lose a friend you didn't have in the first place, she'd done little to gain friends.

Her own fault. Jocey was miserable with the knowledge. From now on, she decided, it wasn't going to be that way! Whether her mouth got fixed or not, she was going to be friendly to everybody. If some wanted nothing to do with her because of the way she looked, so be it. At least she would know she had tried.

With that resolution, Jocey knew a glow of self-satisfaction, a feeling of being at peace with herself, as though she had rounded an important corner in her life. *All right world!* she wanted to shout, *here I am!*

Twice a week now, wearing a clean frock and the navy straw hat with a veil, Jocey took a carload of vegetables, milk, and butter to town. Gram in her newly ambitious state contributed fresh pies and jars of jelly to sell. Making rounds only Saturdays wasn't enough for all that. They were making progress; Jocey felt rich in many ways.

On one trip to town, she spotted a short man in a striped suit strutting the sidewalk ahead of her. Her heart nearly failed, thinking it was Andrew Smith. In that moment she knew she still wanted the operation very much. Especially if Papa was coming home. It would be such a happy surprise for him. The man, when Jocey caught up with him, didn't look like the sewing machine salesman at all. Andrew Smith had probably vanished forever, she realized. For a few minutes, she felt ill from disappointment.

Tom Thunder-Dog showed up at the house again, one late summer day. Hopefully, Jocey asked him if he had seen Andrew Smith on the road anywhere. The Indian peddlar seemed jealous of others in the selling business, and he wouldn't talk about the sewing machine salesman.

One day, Jocey took courage and asked one of her vegetable customers, Mrs. York, as they stood on the woman's porch, if she knew Kipper and Smith. And when they might come back to the valley. She wasn't ready for the fireworks her simple question set off.

"Those shysters!" As she spoke, Mrs. York's thin fingers snaked into the basket Jocey held and she pinched a tomato, squirting juice, making Jocey duck back. "I hope I never see the likes of them again, talking poor folks into buying machines they don't have the money for!"

"People ought to know if they can't afford—" Jocey began.

"Lots of folks around here"—the woman cut her off—"are going to lose their shirts, their farms, even, if they don't stop buying fancies on credit." She snapped a carrot in two. Her nose twitched rabbit-like as she sniffed it. She looked pleased that it was fresh. "Some of the menfolk," Mrs. York went on, "have ordered their wives to send their sewing machines back to the company. Word is out. Those fancy talkers, Kipper and Smith, better not show their faces in these parts again!"

Jocey finished the transaction with a heavy heart. She hoped Mrs. York was wrong, all wrong. She wanted Andrew Smith to come back. One way or another, she wanted to know about the operation.

One afternoon Jocey was stowing hay in the barn. She'd spent a long morning pitching hay from the field into her cart and driving it to the barn to unload. It was tedious work, and she was hot and tired. Taking a rest, she happened to look out the hayloft window, and she saw a dust cloud on the road. It advanced at a good clip. Her heart began to hammer as she waited. As though pulled by her wish, the buggy turned from the road onto her lane.

In minutes the buggy was drawing up at the back porch. A man got out. *Andrew Smith.* Without a doubt. Jocey let out a warwhoop, "Yeeehaaa!" Then she began to tremble.

What if there could be no operation? Her stomach turned over, perspiration broke out fresh on her face. What if the word was *no.* Involuntarily, she covered her ears with grubby calloused hands and ducked down, so as not to be seen at the hayloft window. As though driven, she burrowed deeper and deeper into the fragrant hay.

Below the loft window, Gram called, "Joeee—?"

Jocey stayed where she was, hardly able to

breathe, her heart a hollow ache while tears flooded her face. Then she sat up and wiped the stickery strands of hay from her wet cheeks. Would Andrew Smith come back if the answer was no? He must be here to tell her—*yes!* She gulped back her sobs. Whichever way it was, she had to know. Once and for all.

She whirled down the ladder from the loft, screaming, "Mr. Smith, don't go! I'm here, I'm here. I'm coming, Grandma, I'm coming. Mr. Smith, wait for me!"

CHAPTER 12

Outside the barn Jocey's steps slowed, and her mouth dried. She felt turned to wood all over. Gram and Andrew Smith waited in the back yard.

"Get a hurry on!" Gram motioned to her. "Mr. Smith's come to see you. When you didn't answer me, I thought you'd gone to the Pladsons. But Mr. Smith said he wouldn't leave till he got to talk to you, personal."

Jocey halted a few steps away. She caught her trembling hands together in a painful clench behind her back and crossed her fingers.

"What's all this about, Joee?" Gram demanded with a laugh. "Mr. Smith here acts like a bear just found a honey tree."

She looked directly at him then and found smiles wreathing his face. "It can be done, Missie. I found it out for sure. It isn't common yet, but there is an operation for harelip."

Jocey swayed. All the years of hiding, running, and hurting were to end? She closed her eyes and in a choked whisper she asked, "For real, honest, certain?"

"What is this? What operation?" Gram asked in alarm. "What do you want to do to my grandbaby?"

Poor Gram, she must feel mixed-up, hearing this so sudden for the first time. Jocey took a step toward her.

"Can we go inside and talk?" Smith asked. His eyes on Jocey glowed with satisfaction.

"I'll make coffee," Gram said. "I got to know what in hellfire you two are talkin' about." She bustled through the door looking worried.

Smith bowed for Jocey to go in ahead of him.

Her legs shook, although her heart overflowed with joy; taking the steps up to the porch was like climbing a mountain. In the kitchen, she quickly found a chair. "Tell me—" She drew a long breath. "Tell me everything."

"That's what I'm here for." Beaming, Andrew Smith seated himself opposite her. He leaned forward, looking first at Gram with the coffee canister in her hands, then at Jocey. "There is a doctor in Kansas City who does this. He repairs damage to faces—to mouths, ears, to scars, injuries—whatever needs it. He is very good."

"You're talkin' about cuttin', on my Joee!" Gram burst out.

Smith let it go by. "I talked to the doctor myself. Doctor Brendler. He told me it might take more than one operation, because as a person grows, their face changes. But he'll explain all that to you, Jocey."

"You say this Doctor Brendler is in Kansas City? Where, what hospital?" Jocey asked quickly before Gram could take the floor again.

"Downtown Kansas City," Mr. Smith told her, "the new German Hospital. It's on a hill and—"

"But I know where it is! Two years ago, they built it. The German Hospital is close to our old neighborhood, isn't it, Gram? I passed it a lot, delivering laundry." Had this miracle been available to her when she lived at the bottom of the hill from the hospital? And she hadn't known? Did she have to come to the Neosho Valley to hear? Jocey sighed. Life was so twisting and turning a person hardly knew what to expect next.

Aloud, she mused, "I wonder why we never heard before about this? Is the operation brand new?"

Smith shrugged, "No, this type of surgery isn't so new, and that's the sad part. Doctor Brendler says the first known operations for harelip were performed fifty years ago, in Europe. But even here in America it's been done, successfully, too. The trouble is, people don't know about it." He added, with an angry look, "Or they don't care, even if they do know. You see, having a harelip isn't a matter of life or death. You're not sick or in pain in the usual sense, so it's thought you can get by, live with it."

"Now that's a fact," Gram put it. "Unless folks are near to dying, most of 'em don't go near no hospital."

"I understand," Jocey said slowly. "That would explain why the operation seems rare, and why we haven't heard about it till now." Silently, she added, *and who would care, anyway, about a little slum girl with an ugly upside-down vee for a lip—that showed her teeth like she was snarling? Who?* Who, but herself! She cared very much, and she was going to have the operation!

She looked at Gram, knowing it was important to make it clear from the start. "Grandma, if there is this way to fix my face, I'm going to do it. I have to."

Gram shook her head, and she sagged into a chair. "What you two are talkin' about needs studyin'. And how would we go to Kansas City? It would take more'n a week. Nearly killed me gettin' here in the first place. Now we got this farm to look after."

"Jocey could take the train," Mr. Smith told Gram gently. "Maybe you couldn't afford it before and had to come here by cart. But for just one, it wouldn't be terribly expensive to take the train. She can catch the Missouri Pacific in Council Grove and be in Kansas City in half a day. It'd be pretty simple, really."

"After I get there, I'd know my way around," Jocey added. "I know where Union Station is. I know where the hospital is—I could manage easily. Gram, you wouldn't need to go. You could stay and look out for things here until I come back."

Although Gram didn't look convinced, she seemed to be relenting and thinking. Her voice came low, as if to herself. "I didn't never dream a body could do ary a thing about a harelip. It was punishment we was to bear to our graves."

"Excuse me." Smith spoke up suddenly as he searched his pockets. "I had some papers about this, and I seem to have lost them. I'll check in my buggy for them and be right back." He jumped up and hurried out.

After he'd gone, Gram said, "I can see how much you want this operation Mr. Smith knows about, Joee, but it'd take money, likely more money than we'll ever see in our lives."

Jocey smiled. "We have the savings from our crops we sold. That would buy my train ticket and—" She halted, beginning to add in her mind—money for doctors, money to pay the hospital, money for a ticket to Kansas City and back. They didn't have enough! Her heart climbed into her throat in panic. Then, just as suddenly, she relaxed. "Gram, there's your buryin' money we can use!"

"Ah," the old woman sighed. "Ohh, my." Her face sagged as she looked at Jocey. She got up and shuffled to the window where she peered out at Andrew Smith, on his hands and knees in the buggy.

"Grandma," Jocey pleaded, "this is important. You know I wouldn't ask for your money if this operation didn't mean the whole world to me. And I'll pay the money back later, long before you'll need—a funeral."

"There ain't no buryin' money, child," Gram blurted, turning to face Jocey. "Not for the fine funeral I always talked about, not for nothing else, either."

"T-The sock," Jocey protested, stunned. "What about the sock you've kept close to you, under the mattress? Are you saying, Gram, you never did have the money?"

"Oh, I had it," Gram sighed. "Up to a month or so ago. Joee, a man from the county came by one day. You were gone, selling vegetables. This feller showed me that your Papa was behind on paying taxes. If we didn't pay, they was going to take this farm for back taxes and sell it to somebody else. I give him my funeral money, all of it. Anyhow, we're squared with the county."

"But why, Gram why—?"

" 'Cause I didn't want to lose this place. I didn't want to go nowhere else. You been working hard, and it was easy to see you love it here, too. And now

Jim's likely coming back. He'll need a home to come to."

"I meant, why didn't you tell me about this? Why did you keep it a secret? You know how proud I'd be, how much I'd love you—do love you—for doing such a thing." Jocey's throat hurt, and she was fighting tears.

Gram sighed. "I was going to tell you. I don't know why I didn't right that day, but it don't matter. Now you know. And I ain't the only one that's been keepin' secrets. You musta' known something about this here operation Mr. Smith has been talkin' about, but did you say one word?"

Jocey shook her head. Never before in her life had she felt so warm with love and so deeply disappointed all at the same time. What about the operation now?

Andrew Smith came back into the house, and he took his chair again.

"I—I don't know how I could pay for the operation," she told him. "Unless—maybe we could borrow money from the bank, on the farm. No," she answered herself aloud, "I doubt the bank would even listen with Papa not here to agree to it."

"Now, you don't—" Andrew Smith began.

Gram interrupted, "There ain't a thing I can do to get Joee this operation, ain't that a fine howdy-do? Joee's got her heart plumb set on having it, too. This girl," she told Smith, "has give me some of the happiest times of my life."

"Please," Smith begged, "let me get a word in. I'm telling you, ladies, you are worrying for nothing." He went over to Jocey and knelt down in front of her. "Honey, you don't have to pay for this operation. The surgery is being taught to student doctors. They'd come over from the Kansas City Medical College. If you agree to have the surgery, the doctor does it for free, with the others looking on and learning. Do you understand?"

Jocey nodded once again. But the sigh of relief that came all the way up from her toes was short-lived.

"I knew it," Gram cried, "they want my Joee to be guinea pig, don't they? They'll just be practicin' on her like, won't they?"

Jocey looked at Andrew Smith.

"Practicing? Not hardly." He shook his head and smiled. "Doctor Brendler, who would do the surgery, is an expert. They claim he is the best doctor for this surgery in America."

"I'm going to do it!" Jocey said positively. "I'm going to Kansas City to see Doctor Brendler. If he will help me, I'm going to have this operation."

"I think you're right," Gram admitted finally; "maybe you ought to do this, Joee. But are you sure it's safe?" She turned to Andrew Smith.

"Yes, I do. You see, I talked to a few ex-patients

of his. One man's face had been—" he hesitated, then went on, "torn up something terrible in a factory accident. The doctors were able to put his face back together almost as good as new. Yours won't be the first harelip surgery, either, Jocey. Doctor Brendler has done some others and the results have been splendid."

Jocey wasn't aware when her tears had begun, she only knew the warm flood coursing down her cheeks couldn't be mopped away. She accepted the papers Andrew Smith gave her. Among them was a note of introduction she was to present to Doctor Brendler when she got there. "He knows about me?" she asked Smith.

"He knows about you, and he will be expecting you. First, though, you must write to him to tell him when you can be there. He'll need to make arrangements with the Kansas City Medical School so the students will be on hand."

"I can't thank you enough," Jocey said through her tears, "not now, not ever. But I want to, so much."

He smiled. "My thanks will be when I come back in a few months to see how this turns out."

Some hours after the sewing machine salesman had departed, Jocey was still crying and couldn't stop. She tried, when she looked out the kitchen window and saw Thea Pladson, Anne, and the baby

Kari arrive in their wagon. She went to the door and called a shaky, "H-Hello!"

"You know about our Nils?" Mrs. Pladson said in response to seeing the tears on Jocey's cheeks. "No," she remonstrated herself with a shake of her head, "is something else you cry for. Not Nils. That only happen last night. You couldn't know about that already. Not till we tell you."

"Pl-please come in," Jocey said, wiping her eyes. "What is the trouble?"

Thea plodded silently into the kitchen shaking her head, carrying the baby. Anne followed, a slight frown on her pretty face. They sat down.

Jocey wanted to blurt out her news, every last detail of Andrew Smith's visit. But out of courtesy to their guests, plainly upset, she held her own happiness in check.

Gram reached to get more coffee cups out of the cupboard. "What's this about your boy?"

"Nils ran away," Anne blurted, "and it's all *Far's* fault."

"It happen, it finally happen." Mrs. Pladson nodded. "I see it coming a long time. They have terrible argument last night," Mrs. Pladson said. "Edvard just not understand. Nils is a good boy, but he is like my people. The men in my family at home in Oslo are scholars, ministers, and editors of newspapers— like. Not farmers." She shook her head again. "Nils hates farming. Now, he has run away."

"I—I am sorry," Jocey whispered, "but maybe Nils will change his mind and come home."

Anne declared, *"Far* will have to be different with Nils. If Nils comes back and *Far* wants him to stay."

"Is so, I know," her mother agreed with a moan. "Tosten is the easy-going one, bending to his Papa's will not so hard for him. Is harder for Nils. And Edvard! He can be so stubborn with hard head like a brick. This time, I think he see, though. Now Nils has run away, he will see he cannot be so hard on his children." She saw Jocey wiping at her face again and she cried, "My! I carry on so about Nils, I not ask what is troubling you, Jocelyn?" Her mouth pursed with concern. "What is matter?"

Jocey shook her head, laughing out loud at Mrs. Pladson's expression of sympathy. Gram fidgeted, her eyes asking to be the one to tell their good news, and Jocey nodded for her to go ahead.

"—so," Gram finished, "the Kansas City doctors are going to make my Joee better with a nice mouth." She took a long drought of coffee and then banged the empty cup down on the table. "Oh, I know she is going to be the pretty one!" Tears showed in Gram's eyes although she smiled. She hugged herself and rocked back and forth. "I am sorry for blubbering so." She waggled her hands, then. "But I can't help it." She wadded her apron into her eyes to dry them. "I am so happy for my Joee."

Anne blinked at a bank of tears in her eyes. "Jocey, we're glad for you, too."

"Ahh," her mother cried, "Jim Royal, he should know this. He should be here now. He would be so pleased." She started to cry, and in the next second the baby Kari, staring around at them all, commenced to wail, too. "Is epidemic," Mrs. Pladson sobbed laughingly, hugging her baby, "but is good epidemic, no?" She sighed. "For you I am happy, Jocey. For my Nils wherever he is, I am sad and I want to reach out to him and talk to him. I cry for everybody all mixed up."

Jocey got a towel and passed it around the table. They laughed as they took turns using it. She lifted Kari from the mother's broad lap and cuddled the child in her arms, shushing her soft little sobs. "Thank you," she said to Anne and Mrs. Pladson, "for feeling like you do, for me. I will have to leave Gram alone for a while when I go to Kansas City. Would you look in on her as often as you can?"

"*Yah!*" Mrs. Pladson exclaimed. "Is what neighbors are for. I think Edvard will be different about our coming to see you now. He tries to be angry at your father, but it is not so easy anymore. So long ago their trouble over the books happen, he forgetting. Jocelyn, I will ask Edvard to drive you to the train station. You tell us when you are to leave, and he will be here to pick you up. Tosten will help with chores sometimes, too, while you are away."

"It ain't necessary for your man to take Joee to the train," Gram told their friend. "I can see she gets there."

"I know that. But it would be good for Edvard to do this, to do something nice for his neighbor for a change, do you see? A beginning, a new start, like. Please. It help us, too."

Jocey worried that Mr. Pladson would not be agreeable, but Thea seemed sure of her offer, so Jocey nodded. In a moment, Gram, too, agreed. Even if she had to walk every inch of the way to Kansas City, Jocey thought, she would be going. Nothing could stop her now.

When the Pladsons were leaving a short while later, Jocey told them, "I'm thankful for neighbors to count on, and I think members of a family need one another even more. I'm sure Nils will get lonesome for the rest of you, and he will be back soon."

"That's a fact!" Gram agreed.

Mrs. Pladson looked more hopeful. She leaned toward Jocey; and she, surprised, instinctively started to draw away. Then she remembered, she wasn't going to be that way, anymore. Jocey accepted the woman's affectionate kiss on her cheek, then she herself turned and gave Anne a quick squeeze.

"Good luck in Kansas City." Anne smiled.

"Go with God," Mrs. Pladson told her.

CHAPTER 13

Jocey carefully penned a letter to Doctor Brendler, telling him she would arrive in Kansas City at the hospital in two weeks. Then, she sped through one task after another preparing for her trip and the stay at the hospital. Taking turns with Gram, she finished the violet print dress she'd been working on since early summer. She washed, mended, made over, and pressed her other few dresses and undergarments and packed them in her valise.

She virtually stripped her gardens for the last of the produce to sell in the surrounding towns.

In Council Grove one morning, Jocey double-checked the timetable at the train station and bought her ticket to Kansas City. It was her intention to visit the Pladsons next day to tell them her departure time, but that same day going home, she met Tosten riding horseback into town on an errand for his father.

"Is Nils at home?" she asked, after their greeting.

"Not yet." Tosten shrugged. "But if he does come back, I think everything will be all right. You should hear the scorching *Mor* gives *Far* every day that Nils is gone. Maybe she should have stood up to *Far* before this. Anyway, things are changing for the better at our house."

"I'm glad, Tosten."

"I don't suppose you've had any word from your father?" he asked her.

She shook her head. "If he were really coming, I would have thought he would have been here by now. But I don't know how he's traveling; he could be walking for all I know. And I don't know how well he is; he could be very sick again."

There was a moment or two of silence between them, then Tosten said with a gentle grin, "You have some good news of your own, I hear. Anne and *Mor* told me."

It was as though her very soul smiled in return, although her eyes itched with the threat of tears. "Yes. I am leaving for Kansas City this coming Saturday. I bought my train ticket today. Did your Mother tell you that she offered—?"

He nodded. "We will come to get you. What time, Jocey?"

"The train leaves at eight in the morning. I don't for anything want to be late."

"You won't be. See you Saturday morning."

As promised, Tosten and Mr. Pladson were right on time. The sun had not been up long when they arrived, rattling into the yard in their wagon, but Jocey had been up before the sun, with the lark, and ready.

When she went out, the elder Pladson stood by the wagon, stiffly, a semblance of a smile on his face. "Goot morning," he said quickly, as though he'd been rehearsed. He took off his hat to Gram and nodded to Jocey. "We take you to train." Jocey hoped Thea and Anne hadn't had to battle too hard to accomplish this.

"Good morning, Mr. Pladson, Tosten." She turned to Gram, who shoved a basket lunch into her arms. Gram dabbed at her eyes with her apron, then she flapped it at Jocey to go on and get into the wagon. Jocey gave her grandmother a peck on the cheek and a quick hug. Then Mr. Pladson helped her onto the bench in the back of the wagon, next to Tosten.

They started down the lane. "Goodbye, Gram, take care!" Jocey looked back and continued waving until her grandmother was only a speck in front of the tiny farmhouse. Then she faced forward for the trip through the valley to Council Grove.

After a bit, Jocey thought to nudge Tosten and whisper, "Nils?"

The boy grinned and nodded that Nils was home again. He motioned with his head toward his father and patted the area of his heart to show that his father was softening as his mother had predicted.

Little was said on the way to town through the early morning sunshine. Jocey's head and heart were too full of expectations about what lay ahead of her, and Tosten seemed to know that and to understand.

At last they reached Council Grove, where they drove straight to the depot. Jocey got down from the wagon with Edvard Pladson's help. She was thrown off guard for a second when his hard paw shot out to take hers. For a long moment he held her hand, but not shaking it as he would a man's or a boy's.

From under the veil of her navy straw hat, Jocey smiled up at him, her fear and dislike of him dissipated. "Thank you very much for bringing me to the train, Mr. Pladson. Sir, I hope we will be better neighbors to each other when I come home. I'll do my best."

He grunted softly. The grin that cracked his face this time seemed more genuine.

From the train steps, Jocey waved and called to Tosten, "I'll write to all of you and let you know when I can come home. Take care of my Gram for me, please. Ride Nappy if you want. If Opal and Don Juan get out, they'll be in trouble with the foxes, so—" she stopped. The train was chuffing so loud, and besides, her voice was giving out. " 'Bye, Tosten!"

"I'll be seeing you, Jocey!"

She ran into the car, found a seat, and leaned back, her lunch basket gripped hard in her hands. Tears squeezed out from under her closed lids, she blindly kicked with her toe to make sure her valise was at her feet, and her spirits soared. She was on her way—to a new face, a new life. She echoed silently Mrs. Pladson's prayer, *God be with me.*

In Kansas City, Jocey got out of the throng around Union Station as quickly as she could. She thought about taking a streetcar, but the walk to the stately brick hospital on the hill was not too long.

She set out. When she was a block or two away from the shanty she had shared with Gram, the old chant rang ghostlike in her mind:

> *"Harelip,*
> *Ugly Crip—"*

Jocey felt a spasm of pain, and her face warmed. She walked fast, gripping the handle of her valise, looking about, half-expecting to see The Chasers.

Then she laughed out loud and waved off their ghosts. "Just wait," she called in a choked whisper. "Just wait."

Down the street, a few minutes later, she saw a figure that reminded her of Papa, going into Mr. Porter's, Gram's old landlord's house. She hesitated a second, then dismissed the man; much too old to be Papa.

Papa. For a long time she had wondered if he loved her. Not any more. Papa'd had his own reasons for being away so much. Sometimes a reason could be easily explained, and sometimes it could not. It just *was.*

Papa loved her in his own way. For example, she thought, the books he had brought her from his travels. Never a doll. A book. She knew now why that was. Dolls, every last one, had pretty, rosebud, perfect mouths. She did not. Seeing the terrible difference would surely have made her feel worse, Papa would believe.

At the same time, Papa had known, even before she had found it out for herself, that reading was a passkey into wonderful lives, wondrous times. Books were a *place* where she could be most anything or anyone. Beautiful, if that's how the story went. Or strong and adventurous. Silly, sometimes. Courageous or intelligent. "Thank you, Papa," she whispered as she walked along. "Thank you always, wherever you are."

The hospital neared, and Jocey suddenly felt very alone. But she would not turn back. Not now.

"You came alone?" Doctor Brendler clasped his hands on the desk before him, and he smiled at Jocey.

"Yes." This was the third time she'd answered the same question. The woman at a counter in the hospital's wide entry hall had asked her if she was alone, and so had the black-garbed nun who'd brought her to this small, book-lined doctor's room. Couldn't they see for themselves that there was no one else with her?

Doctor Brendler began to write on a sheet of paper. "We really would prefer to talk to your parents or some other relative."

"I—I thought you might. But that isn't possible. My mama is dead, she died of lung fever when I was little. Papa is—traveling. He's on his way home from Mexico, but he doesn't know about this. My gram had to stay and look after our farm in Kansas. I thought Mr. Andrew Smith told you all about me? And I wrote a letter. Anyway, like I told the nurse-lady in that other office, it's *my* face that needs help."

The doctor's eyes came up slowly and appraised Jocey. Then he came around the desk to where she sat. He lifted the hat and veil from her head and gently took her face into his hands. He tilted her chin back and bent for a closer look. Under his touch, Jocey trembled.

"It's all right." His voice, coming from behind a thick beard and moustache, calmed her. "Open your mouth, dear." She did so, and in a moment he looked up, seeming satisfied. "No cleft in the roof of your mouth, only the lip is involved. That makes our work a lot easier." His hands dropped.

Jocey murmured, "Y-You will do the operation, then?"

"You want this surgery very much, don't you?" Doctor Brendler smiled at her. He sobered then and spoke as if to himself, "Nobody can really know, not even me, a doctor, what you've been through. Can we?"

She whispered, "No."

He went back to his chair shaking his head. "It's so difficult for a person whose face is marred. Too often they suffer far worse rejection than amputees. Or the blind or deaf. A face, especially, is supposed to be—*nice*." He mused, "I know of people with facial disfigurement who went into hiding. Became, literally, recluses all their lives rather than face the rejection and abuse their handicap wrought. Have you found it true, Jocelyn, that your disfigurement itself doesn't bother you so much as the way people respond to it?"

She thought immediately of The Chasers, who had

for so long treated her as a freak and their own special victim. She thought of school, where she was bumped aside in the halls and books were knocked from under her arms; where she'd been the object of vile names and laughter as if she couldn't hear, or was stupid and of no account. How much she had hated all of it! But she didn't want to remember that. Why couldn't they go on to the future? "Will you tell me about the operation? I—I don't know what's going to happen."

"We'll have a long talk about it," he assured her. "First, let's ring for a sister, though, and have her find you a bed and bring you some refreshment. There will be a few more forms she will want to fill out about your medical history, as much as you can tell us. When you're ready, I'll come to see you."

Within minutes, a tall nun with a plain but pleasant face came into Doctor Brendler's office. "Sister Louise, this is Jocelyn Royal. She will be with us for a few days. Will you make her comfortable and call me when she's ready?"

"Jocelyn?" Sister Louise picked up Jocey's valise. "Shall we go? We have a room all ready for you." Her free hand, smooth and cool, caught Jocey's. As she led the way down the long hall, she said comfortingly, "Everything is going to be all right. All of us in this hospital have one aim, and that is to make people well and whole. We take the best care of them that we can while our patients are here."

Jocey sighed. The sound of it was noisy, like a small child's sigh. The nun laughed softly; and Jocey felt even more embarrassed, but she felt better, too.

The high-ceilinged room was spotlessly white and sparsely furnished. Sister Louise helped her into a simple white muslin gown; then she folded Jocey's things neatly back into her valise. "You'll get these back almost before you can say 'jumping beans.' Into bed now." Seated in a chair by the bed, Sister Louise asked Jocey several more questions, about mumps, measles, and so on, and if she'd had them. She wrote Jocey's answers on a paper.

When she was finished, Sister Louise said, "I'll bring Doctor Brendler, now. You know, Jocelyn, he can make your mouth sweeter and prettier than you can know. I've cared for many of his patients, and I've seen him do miraculous work. With God's help, of course."

Jocey nodded to show that she knew she was one of the lucky ones. But if it hadn't been for Andrew Smith, coming to try and sell her and Gram a sewing machine, she probably would never have heard of Doctor Brendler. She'd buy one of Smith's machines as soon as she could!

"How's Miss Royal?" Doctor Brendler stuck his head in the door later. He came and caught her wrist in his hand and waited—doing nothing else—but he looked thoughtful. Surely he knew she was still breathing?

"I'm all right, aren't I?" she whispered huskily.

"As far as I know, you are a very healthy girl. Good pulse, strong heart, and a lot of gumption, too, I'd guess. Now then"—he pulled the bedside chair up closer—"most of tomorrow we will be giving you some checkups of one sort and another. Tomorrow night you will get a good night's sleep. We've been prepared for you, and Monday morning early, we'll take you to surgery."

"Th-that s-soon?"

He laughed. "Want to put it off? Did you change your mind?"

"No!" She shook her head and laughed back up at him.

"Good." His face grew serious. "Now, the actual procedure for repairing the fissure—the harelip—is a meticulous and accurate suturing, or sewing, of the separated tissues, layer by layer. It will take us a while. We want not only the outside skin surfaces stitched together, you see, but the underlying tissues, too. Do you understand?"

"That much I do," she said through a dry throat. She watched his face, her eyes wide.

"So far, so good." He continued, "Good healthy flesh like yours begins to heal rapidly. We don't foresee any trouble there. But you'll be here in the hospital almost a week after the surgery. Then you can go home with instructions for a doctor near you to see if you need further care. I'll take a peek at my handiwork a day or so after. Your face will be red and swollen some, in the beginning. You will feel some pain at first, but that will gradually lessen. I think, all things considered, that you are going to like the results very much. Do we go ahead with it?"

Such a useless question. "I want the operation, Doctor Brendler, more than anything."

When he had gone, Jocey settled back into the curiously smooth bed to wait. She wished she had brought a book to read. Next time she saw Sister Louise, she would ask if there were any books in the hospital.

Something thumped at the door, and a different nun, one with dark, furry brows, strode into the room carrying a tray of steaming food. Then, as if Jocey were a rag doll, she yanked her up into sitting position and plumped the pillows behind her back.

"Th-thank you." Jocey looked at the coddled eggs, dry bread, and tea. It hardly looked worth touching. But she would eat it, because she was hungry, and because she wanted to be as helpful as she could to these people trying to help her.

"Every bite!" The nun gave Jocey a last command before her long black skirts swished out the door.

That first night, Jocey lay awake for hours staring up at the far dark ceiling of her room. Outside in the hall, she heard the occasional soft *pad pad* of the sisters' footsteps coming and going. Someone cried. That patient needed someone to talk to them, Jocey thought, someone to care. She considered getting out of bed and going to find them, but she was afraid she might be breaking a hospital rule if she did.

She wouldn't mind having someone of her own to care, close by. Gram, or Papa. Jocey held back tears. Sister Louise was nice, and she would be with her Monday, when she had the surgery.

Next day, Sunday, Jocey got little rest as one nun or another, or Doctor Brendler and the student doctors, came and went. They came to view her mouth, to hear her chest, and to take her temperature. She was bathed, her bed was changed. *Now they did not want her to eat.* The chloroform she must take next morning to put her to sleep would make her much sicker if she had food now, they told her.

The day passed. More used to her surroundings this second day and comfortable from the kind attention, Jocey slept that night as sound as if she were back on the farm.

Monday morning and the flock of nuns were back, bathing her again, and giving her the medication to make her sleepy. When she breathed in the medication from a cone, Sister Louise said, "You'll be sleepy in a few minutes, now. Why don't you lie quiet and think of something nice—somebody you know, or some place that is special to you. A quiet, rippling stream, maybe?"

Jocey tried to say, "Gram," but her tongue was feeling thick. She pictured Gram's wrinkly face and held that in her mind, until, in a while, Gram's wrinkles turned into plowed fields. She saw young green corn then and husky potato plants and cabbages by the row. Jocey tried to pull her mind away. She saw Tosten with a fistful of posies, then Tom Thunder-Dog, and Andrew Smith who seemed to be shouting encouragement to her. Papa, she saw, too, but his face was blurry and wouldn't come clear. She was so very, very sleepy.

CHAPTER 14

Jocey was waking up. Odd, she thought, but the separation in her lip had never hurt before, bad though it looked. Her face felt strangely stiff, too. She hoped a trouble hadn't arisen that would postpone the surgery. It must be getting close to time for it. Feeling groggy, she started to turn onto her side, but the pain *that* caused in her face made her stay where she was. Her stomach heaved, and she was afraid she might be sick.

What was this? Why did her face feel so funny, as if there was thick dried shaving soap all over it? She reached up and found the bandage. A lot of soft bandage. Even then it took a moment for full realization: the operation was over. Finished, and she hadn't known anything about it!

Jocey tried to call out and found she couldn't speak. But she had to know if the operation worked. She wanted Sister Louise! She had to know if her mouth was fixed the way Doctor Brendler wanted it to be. Her shaking hand found the small bell on the bedside table. She jangled it once, then it slipped from her grasp and rolled tinkling and clattering across the wood-planked floor.

"Sounds like a circus in here!" Sister Jessica swept in. "What do you need? And why are you awake? You're supposed to be sleeping."

Jocey pointed to her bandaged face with one hand and lifted the other palm in question.

"The surgery went fine, of course." Sister Jessica retrieved the fallen bell and returned it to the table. She smoothed Jocey's covers and pillow. In the way they were always doing it, she took Jocey's wrist and held it a moment. She then checked the bandage on Jocey's face. "Everything is all right there. Keep your hands away," she warned.

Before the nun could get out the door, Jocey motioned and tried to speak, to tell her that her stomach was upset.

Sister Jessica frowned. "There's a chamber pot by your bed in case you need it to be sick in, but let's hope that doesn't happen. We're going to have problems with your bandage, but we'll manage if necessary."

Jocey lay back, signaling that she was fine for the moment.

Sister Jessica had hardly departed when Doctor Brendler came. Jocey struggled to sit up and talk. "Mum-m—" she began, wanting to ask about her mouth.

"Now settle back, Jocelyn. The operation went splendidly. How's the pain?"

She motioned that it was of no account. As a price for a dream come true, she didn't mind at all. "Mum-m. S-s-s—?" She pointed to her face.

"You want to see it? Nothing doing my girl, not yet." He laughed. "Let's give the incision a little time to start healing; we want it left sterile—can't touch it." He gave her shoulder a pat. "You'll see my artwork soon enough. Promise me you'll just lie quiet now and rest?"

Everyone wanted her to sleep. But how could she with her stomach heaving and with them coming in to check on her time and again? Yet in spite of her doubts, Jocey slept that afternoon for several hours. She opened her eyes only once, when Sister Louise tiptoed in to take her temperature.

Next day, Doctor Brendler, Sister Louise, and several young men that Jocey now knew were medical students came. All of them peered intently at her exposed mouth, and when Jocey tried to move her lips to ask for a looking glass so she might see, too, Doctor Brendler warned, "No, no! Don't try to talk."

"You mustn't be in too big of a hurry," Doctor Brendler continued to scold mildly, as he examined her face, touching it here and there. "Ah," he crooned, "ah, yes." He turned then to speak to the students, using terms Jocey couldn't begin to understand. In undertones, they asked questions. None of it made sense to her.

Was her mouth all right, or not? Jocey wondered frantically. She made a plea, half squeal, half whimper, "M-m-m—?"

"No." Doctor Brendler shook his head. "You may not see it. The incision looks good to us at this stage," he said as he rebandaged it, "but it might worry you. Too early. Time, dear, now you must give this a little time."

All right, Jocey decided, finally. She would bear the waiting, everything, somehow. But she wanted so much to see, to know if—

Each morning, for the next four days, Doctor Brendler and Sister Louise changed the bandage with the others looking on. But they would not let Jocey have a mirror. She began to feel like the guinea pig Gram had spoken about. Wrinkles would furrow the doctor's forehead as he examined her mouth. Whether his frown was from concentration or worry, Jocey couldn't decide. But dread settled in her heart and started to grow.

These are good people, Doctor Brendler, Sister Louise, and the others, Jocey thought. *But they are only mortals and they can't give me a new mouth. No living soul can perform such a miracle. I haven't any right to expect it. I want too much.*

A warm, husky voice interrupted her downhearted thoughts, and feelings. "Jocelyn Royal? If this don't beat all. You under that bandage, is you Jocelyn Royal?"

A black woman in a blue dress, her arms filled with folded sheets, stood in her doorway. Jocey recognized Mary Jordan, the laundress she and Gram had turned their laundry route over to before leaving Kansas City for the farm. "M-Mary—H'lo—" Jocey got out. She motioned the woman to enter her room. Gram would love to hear how the widow Mary Jordan was doing, and all about the people on the old route. She would never forgive her if she didn't ask. Mary must work for the hospital now, she realized, as a ward maid and laundress.

Mary came in slowly. "The chart on your door says you is Jocelyn Royal. I just saw it today as I was walking by. You is Letty Stern's grandchile, ain't you?"

Jocey nodded. She attempted to smile under the bandage, but the pain quickly stopped her. Instead, she waggled her fingers in a friendly, acknowledging gesture.

"Did your daddy bring you in here?" Mary asked,

plumping down into a chair. "You gettin' that poor little mouth of yours fixed, ain't you?"

"My fath—er is—Mum-Mexico," Jocey told her carefully.

"No, he ain't. Not 'less he's a fast traveler. He's right here in the neighborhood if he ain't left already for Kansas."

Right here? In Kansas City? In America all ready? Somehow she'd taken it for granted it would be a long, long time. Her heart began to swell with excitement. Papa, *here?* "D-did you s-see him?" she managed to ask Mary. "Did you see Pa-pa, your-self?"

"Sure as my name is Mary." The woman slipped out of a shoe and commenced to massage her stock-inged foot. "Anyhow, this gent come around the neighborhood a few days ago. I never met your pappy myself. But this man says he's 'looking for Missus Letitia Stern and his child, Jocelyn Royal.' He told my man he come from far to find you, but you was gone, took off."

It was true then, Papa *was* here! Jocey could hardly breathe; her heart pounded furiously. She propped herself up on her elbows. Ignoring the pain and stiffness in her lip, and as though life depended on it, she spoke clearly, "I want Papa. Can your man-friend find him? Bring him—here."

At sight of the tears wetting Jocey's bandage, Mary leaped to her feet and got her shoe back on.

"Don't get yourself upset, hon," she cried. "I'll send Louis to look for your daddy. But you got to stop bawling, honey, please." She hustled for the door. "Oh, my head gonna' roll for bothering this girl."

Jocey listened to Mary's footsteps fade away down the corridor. For the next hours, she fidgeted in near breathless suspension. She wished they'd let her go look for Papa herself. She could find him, if he was in the old neighborhood. What if Mary or her friend couldn't find him? Papa might have left for the farm, he might be right there now with Gram. That, she decided, would be all right. But he mustn't go away again, not before she could see him, talk to him, be with him.

Late that evening, a noise in the hallway made Jocey look up. A thin, worn-out looking man was in her doorway. Across her mind flickered the image of the old man she'd seen pass into Mr. Porter's house. Could Papa's sickness have done this to him? For here, in a rumpled brown suit, his hair mostly gray, was the same man—and a faded imitation of Papa.

He smiled at her, and suddenly he was Papa. Papa for real. "Jocey, are you all right?" He crossed the floor slowly, his smile damp. "It has been a long time. You look grownup, lying there, a big girl, so much taller."

"P-Papa. I'm so glad you've come back. How are you?"

"I'm fine, Jocey. I brought you a book. Do you still like to read?"

"Always, Papa."

He brought the book to her then, and he held her in his arms for a long, long while. Both of them began to shake with quiet tears. Then Jocey whispered, "Papa, do you know why I'm here?"

He sat back, his hands clasping her shoulders, and he nodded. "They kept me at the office awhile. I talked to Doctor Brendler. Jocey, this is so wonderful, I just can't tell you how I feel. I ought to've been here with you all along. I'm sorry, honey, you had to go through it alone."

"You came at the right time, Papa."

"No. I wanted to come home long ago. In my heart and soul I have been ready, but the rest of me wasn't. Physically, I wasn't able to be moved. Jocey, sweetheart, there's so much for us to talk about, so many years to cover. I finally got well enough to come and take you and your grandmother out to the farm at last, then I found when I got here that you'd gone on without me. I'm happy you did. I was going there myself, leaving tomorrow. I was pretty worn down, and Mr. Porter was letting me rest for a few days at his house."

"You'll like it on the farm now, Papa. It's truly the most wondrous place." She thought to ask, "Papa, will you be here with me, please, when they —they take the bandages off for good?"

He smiled gently. "I intend to be. Wild dogs couldn't keep me away. Doctor Brendler says your big day is tomorrow, and he's already said I can be beside you. Nothing to worry about, sweetheart."

They talked all the rest of the evening, about the farm, about Papa's bad time in Mexico, about Gram, about a thousand different things it seemed to Jocey. Papa wouldn't leave her that night, until the nuns grew quite angry and made him go. In the morning, early, he was back, with Doctor Brendler, Sister Louise, and the ever-present young medical students. Everyone was uncommonly quiet today, and they moved with stiff, awkward motions, Jocey thought.

Without preamble, Doctor Brendler began to snip away Jocey's bandage with delicate silver scissors. Jocey's eyes frantically found Papa's gentle face. Her throat dried to parchment. Papa came nearer, taking her hand as the bandage fell away.

She swallowed, and she closed her eyes for a second or two. Then, with deep intensity, she tried to see her answer in the faces gathered around her. Like chalk statues, everybody was straight-faced, hiding their reaction. So she might see and decide for herself, that must be why, she decided. Poor actors. Though her vision blurred, Jocey caught a twinkling eye here and there; a smile nudged at this mouth and that. It was all right then. All right.

Her heart fluttered within her chest like a bird wanting escape when Papa took the looking glass from Sister Louise to give it to her. Her glance darted instantly to her reflection. Jocey sucked in a quick small breath. She looked and looked. Her face was swollen yet; around the incision her dark tan skin was the color of brick. But the awful gap was closed, neatly, beautifully closed. Some, seeing the swelling and redness, the stitches, might think her ugly still. But she knew better. With practiced imagination she pictured away all that. "It's come true," she whispered mostly to herself. "It's come true."

Like a beehive had been suddenly set down in the room, everyone began to talk at once.

"What do you think, honeybun?" Papa's grin was eager.

"Didn't I tell you?" Sister Louise said.

Doctor Brendler, beaming, mocked, "All our work and we get no thanks? You'll have a fine scar for a while, but that will soon fade . . ."

"It—I—me—" she stammered. *I am beautiful.* The words were her gratitude, her heartfelt thanks. "Papa"—she looked at him—"Gram always said I was pretty, that I look like Mama, but I think she's going to be surprised. When can we go home?"

Author's Note

Jocelyn Royal and the events in this book are imaginary, as are the other characters. Behind the story are these facts: One child in every seven hundred is born with a cleft lip and/or cleft palate. The familiar term "harelip" refers this facial disfigurement's similarity to a hare or rabbit's mouth.

A harelip occurs during development of the embryo when the two sides of the upper lip fail to fuse together. Yet for years superstition prevailed about the cause. A pregnant mother touched a rabbit, saw the moon eclipse, had a severe fright of some sort, or *passed a butcher shop with rabbit carcasses strung in the window.*

A German surgeon, Von Graefe, and Roux, a Parisian surgeon, describe methods of harelip closure as surprisingly early as the 1820s. A daring and skillful Scottish surgeon, William Ferguson, in the years 1830 to 1837 performed eight operations for the congenital deformity of harelip—all eight repairs termed successful.

Still, it is unfortunately true that for many years harelip surgery was considered unessential, because the patient was not in danger of death. Little if any thought was given to the patient's psychological and social well-being. Today, a harelip in most cases would be repaired even before the new infant leaves the hospital following birth. The eventual result being a barely visible hairline scar.

I used many and varied sources to write Jocey's story. The towns and cities mentioned are actual places. The hospital where Jocey went for her surgery actually existed. It was established in 1886 by a group of German-American citizens of Kansas City. Today it is the Truman Medical Center, a teaching hospital, part of a large complex of hospitals and schools popularly called, "Hospital Hill."

—*Irene Bennett Brown*